WITCH IN PROGRESS

A BLAIR WILKES MYSTERY

ELLE ADAMS

D1603658

To be notified when Elle Adams's next book is released and get a free short story, *Witch at Sea*, sign up to her author newsletter.

T he phone call offering me my dream job didn't exactly get off to a flying start.

The sound of a ringtone cut through my hangover in the early hours of the morning, on the twenty-something day of this latest bout of unemployment. I grabbed my phone from the bedside table, wincing when the bright sunlight through the blinds glanced off the screen. A cheery voice as bright as the sun spoke into my ear. "Miss Blair Wilkes?"

I pictured the speaker as a young blond woman with a friendly smile, but in my mind's eye, the image warped, turning into a hairy face with long, sharp teeth. Whoa. I'd really overdone it last night.

"That's me," I said, in response to her question.

"I have great news! You have the job."

"That's... great." Ah. I'd applied for dozens of jobs in the last week alone. If it sounded vaguely like I'd be qualified, I was first at the door. And, to be honest, usually first *out* the door. "Can you be a little more specific? Who's calling?"

"Dritch & Co," she said sunnily.

I cast my mind around in an attempt to recall which application she'd responded to. Somewhat tricky given that I'd perfected the art of filling out seven application forms at once and could become an expert on any subject in ten minutes courtesy of Google. But nothing about this "Dritch & Co" rang any bells in my hangover-ridden skull.

"Erm," I said. "I believe I applied a while ago… I may have forgotten the details."

Probably true. The other week, I'd got a call from a coffee shop I'd applied to when I was eighteen and they'd seemed genuinely nonplussed that I'd actually aged in the last seven years and they couldn't pay me the under-21s minimum wage. I blamed the robots for setting unrealistic expectations.

"It's a paranormal recruitment firm in the town of Fairy Falls."

A what *recruitment firm?* Apparently the wine had messed up my hearing as well as my mental functions. I'd thought recruitment firms usually hired graduates, but it wasn't outside the realm of possibility that I'd applied to one of those positions in the hope that nobody would glance too closely at my graduation date. Maybe I'd misheard the rest of it. I was starting to think I hadn't sobered up yet.

"You're exactly what we're looking for," she said. "When Veronica saw your profile, she knew we had to have you."

Profile? I'd uploaded my pitiful employment history to approximately five hundred recruitment sites since I'd been a bright-eyed graduate. At twenty-one, everyone wanted me. At twenty-five, I'd pretty much burned through every possible employer in the town and quite a few in the next town over, too. Despite my dozy state, suspicion filtered in. There was usually a catch. And had she said *Fairy* Falls?

"So I've been invited to an interview, or…"

"No, you've got the job."

"But…" What? Surely I needed to go through an interview at the very least. For one thing, I had absolutely no clue what this job was all about. Or *where* it was. "Fairy Falls? Did I hear that right?"

"It's a little out of your way. But the job's yours." She beamed. I blinked in confusion, not so much because of her words but because she wasn't on video and I hadn't actually seen what her face looked like. Yet the image in my head of a smiling blond woman reappeared, warping into the hairy-faced monster again.

You're dreaming. I pinched my arm, hard. Ow. Now my arm hurt as well as my head. My mouth tasted like something had curled up and died in it.

"I'll send you some more information via email," she went on. "We're looking for fresh blood… don't worry, we're not vampires. Not me, anyway."

I tried for a laugh but didn't quite get there. Mostly because my brain wouldn't stop showing me images of fangs and hairy faces. I definitely needed to stay away from the heavy stuff. I didn't even drink that often—being penniless disqualified me from the swanky bars my former classmates frequented—but I'd been invited to an engagement party for my last unmarried friend from my year group at school and had accidentally ended up reliving my undergrad days.

Wait a moment. I'd been out last night because it was a Friday. What kind of firm called new potential employees on a Saturday morning? Evidently, the same type of company who operated from a town with a name like *Fairy Falls,* made jokes about vampires, and had possibly said the word paranormal.

My phone pinged as an email showed up with a map attached. This Fairy Falls was located some five miles from here in the middle of Cumbria.

My brain screeched to a halt as the improbability of the

situation hit me. Unless you had connections, most jobs had an interview or two. I'd only got my last bar job because I'd bribed a friend into pretending I was their long-lost cousin. And then I'd had an unfortunate and violent sneezing fit while polishing cutlery.

"Is there anywhere I can find accommodation?" I asked the woman on the phone. "I don't live close enough to commute."

If I'd been offered a job anywhere else, finding temporary accommodation would have been a minor consideration. But I'd never heard of this town. It sounded vaguely touristy. Actually, that was a good explanation for the weird name. Maybe I'd be dressing up in medieval-style clothes to take tourists around England's rainiest corners. I could do that.

"You're in luck," she said. "I understand this location is difficult to find, and one of your colleagues has offered to send you a link to somewhere you can find accommodation. If it all works out well, you'll start Monday morning."

My email pinged again.

"I…" *Use your words, Blair.* "Thank you." Until reality decided to pay another visit, I might as well check my inbox.

Hello Blair, said the email, which came from someone called Bethan. *This is my friend, Alissa. She's looking for a flatmate. If you're interested, I can put you in touch with her. She's easy-going, loves animals, and is a member of the Meadowsweet Coven.*

I had zero clue what that last part meant, but if the email footer was any indication, the message came from one of my new co-workers. I scrolled down. Maybe there was another Blair Wilkes they'd meant to contact. Someone with the same name as me. And, apparently, the same email address.

I opened the link attached to Alissa's name. She was a real person, as far as the social networking sites went. Then I searched for my co-worker, Bethan. She was real, too.

I ran a hand over my face, put the phone aside and took two painkillers before returning to the generous flat share offer. If I had only one day to find somewhere to live, then my options were limited. Usually I took the first available spare room, which explained why right now, I was living in the same house as a half-dozen eighteen-year-old students who occasionally held house parties right underneath my feet. It wouldn't be the first time I moved to a new town where I didn't know anyone and crossed my fingers that I hadn't accidentally signed up to live with a serial killer.

I opened the link to the site where they'd apparently found my details. My profile was there. Photo. Contact details. Entire sorry job history, embellished with fancy words to make me sound like a confident career woman. I had no memory of uploading it, but how else had it ended up there? Returning to the email, I skimmed through the details. If I accepted the offer to live with this Alissa person, I needed to pay a month's deposit… Bye bye, savings.

Wait. Was I actually considering taking them up on their offer?

Maybe it was the pounding of my headache, maybe it was the dirty underwear my teenage housemate had left dangling from the window, or maybe it was the fact that my bank account was on the brink of sliding into negative numbers, but I found myself packing my bags within two minutes of the call. Ten minutes later, I'd phoned every person in my contacts I was still on speaking terms with to let them know I was leaving town. Again.

"Did you say *Fairy* Falls?" yelled Rebecca, my best friend.

It was hard to hold a conversation with a screaming infant in the background, hangover or not. "Yes," I shouted back. "I know it sounds bizarre, but they gave me the offer without an interview."

"They're hoaxing you."

"Thanks for being the voice of reason." It seemed too *weird* to be a hoax. "Look, it's not like I can't come back here whenever I want." Within reason. I was paying rent on my room in the shared house, but since my foster parents had retired to spend their days water-skiing in Australia, I had no backup. I *needed* this job.

"Didn't mean to rain on your parade," she said. "Hey, one of us has to make reckless decisions. Hope it works out for you."

She hung up. I shook my head at the phone. To say we'd gone down different paths was an understatement. I might have pointed out that she was the one who'd bought the wine that had resulted in some ill-advised dancing on tables last night, but what would be the point? Maybe a fresh start was precisely what I needed.

I'd never known my birth parents. They'd given me up for adoption when I was a few days old, and I'd bounced between foster homes for a bit before Mr and Mrs Wilkes had taken me in. They loved me like real parents, but the rule was clear—when I'd turned eighteen, my allowance was cut off and I was out. They seemed genuinely disappointed that I'd yet to make anything of my life. I didn't begrudge them for enjoying their retirement, but it'd be nice to have someone to see me off to my new job. Even if I ended up returning with my tail between my legs like I usually did.

Maybe it was growing up in foster care, but I'd always felt a dozen steps behind everyone else in my peer group, and that feeling had only intensified as they'd all settled into careers and families. I'd concluded that everyone else had clearly been handed a guidebook to life at birth and I'd missed out on it. And now here I was, single, alone, without a steady form of employment, and this mysterious job offer was a lifeline I couldn't afford to lose.

New start. I'd better not screw up this one.

———

The first bus driver laughed at me outright when I asked for a ticket to 'Fairy Falls'. With the second, I asked for a ticket to the next village over. Then the bus broke down. The driver got out and walked away, leaving me as the only remaining passenger. I waited five minutes, realised I was going to be late for my induction, and disembarked with my suitcase, following Google maps. Even my phone didn't think the town existed.

The problem with snap decisions is that when they go wrong, you have no one to blame but yourself. I didn't know where the nearest bus stop to the village was. Nor the train. Everything seemed to kind of… skip this area of the countryside. Including the roads. No wonder the bus had had trouble. There wasn't even a proper footpath, more of a halfhearted muddy trench between fields. I looked at my phone. No internet connection. No phone signal either. I'd printed a map of the town from the email, but it didn't tell me how to get there.

My suitcase wasn't heavy, but I started to feel the strain after I'd been wheeling it for a while. I'd put most of the things I owned into my rucksack, but that was fairly lightweight too, aside from my second-hand laptop. Long stretches of unemployment had led me to sell most of my material possessions on eBay, and the number of times I'd moved had made me reluctant to hang onto too much. I'd been told my new flat was furnished, but I'd need to arrange for the rest of my things to be delivered to my new address… if I ever found it.

At least the scenery was nice, and this was hardly the first time I'd wound up lost in the middle of nowhere. A lake glittered in the distance between green fields. The bus had driven for an hour, but we were still a while off from the

Lake District, unless I'd walked further than I'd thought. The lake must be a landmark, right? For a moment, I was certain I saw buildings reflected in the water, but they disappeared a second later. I thought mirages only appeared in deserts, not wet and muddy fields.

I slipped and skidded and dragged my suitcase in the direction of the lake. By the time I got close to it, I knew I must have imagined the buildings. There weren't any, just a vast expanse of water. I thought I knew all the lakes in the area, but this one was... distinctive. Its surface shimmered like spun gold, and I glimpsed weird flashes in the water. Almost like faces, with sharp teeth and weeds for hair. I blinked, and they disappeared.

Apparently my grasp on geography was worse than I'd thought. And quite possibly my grasp on sanity, too. Everything since that phone call had been like a waking dream. I turned my back on the lake, checking my phone again. Still no signal. The bus had disappeared from view, too. *Oh no.*

I looked around and my heart leapt when I spotted a person standing in the middle of the muddy path leading alongside the lake. Yes! Civilisation. I could ask for directions back to the bus stop. The figure was male, and his stance was... sort of intimidating. I stopped. Fear flooded me. What if he was a murderer or madman? That really should have been my first thought.

He was walking towards me. Oh no.

I gripped my suitcase, ready to ditch it and run for my life. Not that there was anywhere to run aside from the lake, and the houses...

Huh?

Houses stood on either side of me, as suddenly as though they'd popped out of thin air. The mud turned to cobbled streets between brick houses right out of a Victorian novel.

What in the world? The crooked sign saying 'Welcome to

Fairy Falls' which had suddenly appeared at the lake's edge on my right wouldn't have looked out of place in a horror movie.

Oh, god, the man was still walking towards me. At least houses meant there must be other people around, right?

"How did you get here?" he asked. His voice was deep, and he looked even more intimidating close up. Tall, dark, broad-shouldered, and dressed in some weird outdoorsy clothes like he was on the way to hike up a mountain. Oh wow. People who looked like they'd strode out of the covers of a romance novels did not strike up conversations with me. Unless I'd spilt coffee on them or tripped over their shoes.

"I need to see your ID," he said. "If you're new in town."

"I—excuse me?"

"I'm security. This is the border to Fairy Falls. What are you here for?"

"I'm here to start my new job. I have to show identification to get into the town?"

"ID," he said, again. "You shouldn't have been able to find this place if you're an outsider."

"I am an outsider." Was I ever. But his expression didn't yield an inch. My common sense caught up and I fumbled for my provisional driver's licence.

He scanned the picture, recognition flashing across his face. "My mistake. You look younger in the photograph. You're the new girl, right?" He was looking at me like he knew me.

"New girl? I guess I am."

His forehead scrunched up. "You don't sound certain of that."

"I think I know my own name." Except when I occasionally misspelt it on application forms after an all-nighter. "I'm here for a job trial."

"I know. Everyone knows."

"You're not helping the horror movie vibes," I said. "If you're planning to sacrifice me to the ancient god of your mysterious lake, I'm out of here."

He raised an eyebrow. "Ancient god? The merpeople aren't that bad."

Right. Apparently my brain had had another moment and thought he said merpeople. "I meant in horror movies. You know. Like a creepy cult."

"No. I wouldn't say the Meadowsweet Coven are *that* bad, but they own everything here."

"The what coven?" I said blankly.

"I wouldn't say that in front of Madame Grey. In fact, you're probably best to steer clear of her if you're not with one of the local covens, and I'm assuming you're not. I'm also assuming you're not a shifter, but there are certain designated areas for shifting. It's considered bad manners to turn into a wolf in the workplace."

I blinked at him. Whatever weird lingo he was using, I was completely lost, in more ways than one.

He was giving me that look again. I didn't have dirt on my face, did I? I hadn't checked since my desperate departure from the bus, and my pristine appearance when I'd left the house had long since been replaced by frazzled bewilderment. And he still wasn't getting out of the way.

I decided to humour him. "So are you the security guard for the whole town? What do you do, stop these… shifters from wandering in?"

"Amongst other things. I don't kill evildoers anymore… I retired from hunting a long time ago."

My mouth fell open. "Hunting… what?"

"Only the bad things. Not witches. You're safe."

Did he imply…?

Right. The hot security guard might be off his rocker, but I was already here. I had nothing to lose. I'd see how my new co-workers were before I ran screaming for the hills. There was no shortage of hills to run screaming into, given the scenery.

"Want me to escort you to the office?" he asked.

"No, thanks. I mean, shouldn't you be guarding the border? Since you're the only security guard there…"

He couldn't have been standing there waiting for me to arrive, right? It was entirely possible that everyone at Dritch & Co was pranking me by sending me their super-hot security guard before drowning me in the lake or leaving my mutilated body in a nearby field. Except the houses hadn't disappeared. Neither had the sign. *Fairy Falls.* It stood beside the lake, leaning at a crooked angle and making me considerably more reluctant to retrace my steps. The only other way to walk was past the houses, towards the centre of the town.

"I'm sure I'll see you around, Blair," he said.

Only when he'd gone did I realise I hadn't asked him for directions. I pulled the town map from my pocket with shaking hands. I was positive it hadn't had buildings on it before, but there it was—the lake, the town, and Dritch & Co's office, two roads down. I walked past more houses, my suitcase bouncing off the cobblestones. There, on my left. Dritch & Co was a small brick building, unremarkable enough that it blended in with its neighbours—an estate agent and a flower shop. It also seemed to be called *Eldritch & Co*, which sounded more like something out of a H.P. Lovecraft novel than a nice and normal small town in the north of England. But what had I expected, a towering block like in London? Shaking my head at myself, I peered inside. I might as well ask directions to the nearest bus stop from here. Better than walking so close to the lake…

A young woman with curly black hair bounded into view. "I wondered if you'd come here first," she said, beaming. "You must be Blair."

I blinked. Then recognition dawned. I'd seen her picture on the email—Alissa, my new flatmate. She looked nice and normal, but then again, so had the security guard before he started speaking gibberish.

"Hey," I said. "Nice to meet you."

"You too," she said. "I'll take your suitcase back with me. You don't mind cats, right?"

"No, of course not."

"Good. Roald is my familiar. He might take a while to warm up to you, but he's generally friendly with strangers."

Did she say… familiar?

My suitcase wheeled away from me, and I swore it levitated off the ground for a moment—but right then, the door to Eldritch & Co's office opened.

"Is that you, Blair?" called the friendly voice who'd spoken to me on the phone. "Come in."

One of the people in the building must have an explanation. Hoping I hadn't got myself into a mess I couldn't walk away from this time, I entered.

2

At the reception desk, a hairy wolf-like face greeted me. I gasped.

Then I blinked and a blond woman sat in its place, wearing a vaguely puzzled expression. "Is something wrong?"

Yes. I'm losing my mind. "No. You… did I speak to you on the phone?"

"Yes, you did. I'm Callie. Nice to meet you, Blair."

She reached out to shake my hand. I did so as quickly as possible, unable to rid myself of the weird sensation of fur brushing against my palm. She looked exactly like the image that had popped into my head when I'd answered the phone two days ago, but I'd never seen a picture of her before. And I'd been so certain I'd seen a wolf sitting in her place. If I'd consumed some hallucinogens during my wine-induced haze on Friday night, it'd have worn off by now, right? Also, my dreams generally weren't this detailed. Or interesting.

"You're just what we needed," she went on. "You're good at answering phones, right?"

"Absolutely." At least in a job that involved making phone

calls to potential recruits, there were limited opportunities for breaking things. Or sneezing on polished cutlery, come to that.

The door to the left of the reception desk opened and another woman strode in. She held a stack of papers in one hand, a half-filled coffee mug in the other, and had her phone balanced on her shoulder as she spoke into it. "...I'll call you back later. I have a new employee to show around."

The phone flipped into her hand. I blinked, certain she'd been holding papers and a coffee mug a second beforehand, but now she held only the phone and a pen. "You're Blair, right?"

The woman was around my age, with straight dark hair and a friendly smile. I looked surreptitiously around for wherever she'd put the papers, but the only furniture was Callie's desk, several feet away from her. I really was losing my grip.

"Yes, I am," I said, not sure if I was answering her or the voice in my head. I needed to sit down, but a werewolf occupied the only seat. No. Not a werewolf. *Pull yourself together, Blair.*

"I'm Bethan," she said. "I'll show you around, okay? This is bound to be overwhelming at first, but I'm sure you'll get the hang of things quickly."

Overwhelming was one way to describe it. I hesitantly peered into the office, and, seeing no werewolves or disappearing files, I followed Bethan inside.

"This is the main office... you'll be working here." She indicated a desk with a computer and phone. The sight of the computers was oddly reassuring. The town might look like a medieval village on the outside, but everyone wore normal clothes and sounded like they came from the twenty-first century. Except for the weird lingo, that is.

I glanced at my desk. The one beside it—Bethan's—overflowed with so much paperwork, it was a wonder her computer still fit into the space. Files and papers were stacked haphazardly at all angles with brightly coloured markers between the pages.

Bethan cleared the papers to the side. "If you're a neat freak, it's cool. I'll move my stuff."

The papers jumped into a drawer, which closed itself without her touching it.

No you don't. Crack up later. I blinked hard. The papers on my own desk remained static, thank goodness.

I looked at the computer instead. Most offices came with computers at least a decade out of date. These were sleek and shiny, but I didn't recognise the model. The logo on the side resembled a face. A human face, with... fangs. Like an illustration of Count Dracula.

I looked suspiciously at the coffee cup on Bethan's desk, then gave myself a mental shake. Why did the idea of vampires seem more plausible than, say, monster hunters? I blamed *Twilight.*

"That's the interview room," said Bethan, indicating another door at the back. "We sometimes bring clients here to discuss their specific needs. You know how hard it can be to find stable employment when you're one of us."

I stared at her for a moment. *One of... what?* I'd walked into job interviews without reading the full description before, but nothing quite like this. And how had she made the papers move like that?

"Don't keep the new girl all to yourself, Bethan," said the occupant of one of the desks opposite ours. A young woman with warm brown skin and braided hair smiled at me. "I'm Lizzie. You're... Blair, right?"

Her hesitation made some of the missing pieces snap together. They'd done this routine before. I'd been in offices with a high turnover rate and experienced the same thing.

Except this time it might not be down to micromanaging, over-demanding bosses and more to do with the fact that everyone in this town was several cards short of a deck. To say the least.

I cleared my throat. "So you all know who I am? Do you all work weekends, or...?" The email had said I'd be working Monday-Friday, your standard 9-5 hours, so it was doubly weird that I'd got the call on the weekend. Maybe the boss, or the receptionist, was hugely enthusiastic.

"No, of course not," said Bethan. "Why?"

"I got the call on Saturday, and... I guess you've had my details for a while." From the site I'd forgotten I'd uploaded them to. Along with the photo I didn't remember taking.

"No, but everyone knows who you are."

Oh...kay. I spotted movement out of the corner of my eye and dropped my gaze to the desk as more papers slid into view. The topmost one was covered in weird-looking symbols. A chill ran down my back. Had I unwittingly walked into a cult of Satanists? Or a parallel reality? It made no sense—not that they knew me, but that they thought I knew *them.* I didn't even fit into the reality I'd lived in for most of my life, let alone whatever this was.

"Don't freak her out," Lizzie said disapprovingly. "It was Veronica who told us. The boss. She found your details online and passed them on to Callie and the rest of us."

"Yeah, Callie sometimes works weekends," added Bethan. "She's a werewolf. She's making up for lost hours thanks to the full moon."

I was supposed to laugh, right? I managed a kind of nervous titter. "Okay."

"Yes. It's hard for people like her to find employment in other towns, but we aren't like that here. Everything is confidential, including our clients."

Smile and nod. Just smile and nod until the universe flips over and makes sense.

A growling noise from behind Lizzie made me jump.

"Just the printer," said Bethan. "I asked it to print out the basic info for you."

"Asked it?"

"It prefers if you ask nicely," said Lizzie.

Right.

The printer emitted another growling noise, and a jet of paper shot across the room, landing neatly on Bethan's desk.

I stared at it. She picked it up and put it in my hands. I let her, because I was pretty sure the last piece of my sanity had packed its bags and left. "Thank you." Next I'd be thanking the printer.

There was no discreet way to leave this situation. Ninety percent of me was sure that I'd make my excuses at the first opportunity and then make a run for it. Eat the cost of the deposit... I'd have to get another credit card or loan. But that's what I got for gambling on a too-good-to-be-true scenario. And it beat being murdered and thrown in a lake, right?

Who was I even kidding? I took a step towards the door, my foot catching on the swivel chair, which knocked against a partly open drawer. A file had got jammed in it, and I glimpsed the title... *Mr Bayer, searching for a spell-making assistant.* Somehow, I doubted they meant in the national spelling competition sense. I looked at the desk, where a newspaper was folded over, depicting the face of a whiskered man who'd apparently been found dead. I guess crime was as common here in NotNormalsVille as it was anywhere else.

"Oh." Bethan grabbed the file from the drawer and moved it to her own desk. "Sorry. That's from... that's a client we already dealt with. I mean, found a suitable candidate, so the opening is closed."

There came a disparaging noise from behind the desk opposite hers, and the fourth occupant of the office finally looked up. "Nice going, Bethan."

"Blythe," said Bethan, in a warning tone. "Aren't you going to introduce yourself?"

The woman, a pale-skinned brunette, gave me a brief glance. "What's this one called?"

That's polite. "Blair," I said. I might be considering climbing out of the window and making a run for it, but I wouldn't stand for being dismissed, either. "I'm replacing someone, is that right?"

"You might say that," said Blythe. "You're here because we needed a fourth. No other reason."

"*Blythe,*" said Bethan sharply.

"Needed a fourth?" I asked.

"We work better with four of us," said Bethan. "Four witches. But if you decide it's not for you, it's not a big deal. *Some* people don't adapt well to change." She gave Blythe another warning look, but it hardly registered. *Witches.* Plainly they were into some kind of weird New Age stuff. You'd think they'd be a little more professional rather than making wild guesses at my hobbies while at work. On my first day, no less.

The rational part of my mind said that whether they were part of a cult or just plain batty, the things I'd seen—the papers, and the printer—they couldn't easily be explained away. But I was a hundred percent certain they'd got me confused with someone else. Someone with the same name, email address, phone number and job history. It could happen, right? I mean... right?

"So... the last person left? I mean, the person who worked here before me?"

"Yes, she did."

They were scurrying to fill a vacancy. *That* made sense.

But I couldn't deny what I'd seen. Nor the fact that the previous employee had apparently been helping someone called Mr Bayer find a spell-making assistant. That's what they did: supply odd clients with equally odd potential employees.

"She's a *normal,* you morons," said Blythe. "I don't need to be able to read thoughts to tell she's never seen one of us before in her life."

Bethan hitched on a smile. "Please ignore every single word that comes out of Blythe's mouth. Everyone else does, including the clients."

Blythe's eyes narrowed, but Lizzie rose to her feet, waving a short wooden stick. Blythe sank into her seat, making… frog noises?

"I'll take it off when you stop winding up the new girl." Lizzie smiled widely. "Carry on, Bethan."

"This is… a mistake." What I actually wanted to say was, *did you wave a magic wand and cast a spell on her?*

I wasn't completely dense. I'd read all the Harry Potter books and grew up reading fantasy tales. This office might look a long way from an ancient castle, but it wasn't like I had no frame of reference. On the other hand, I might have to toss those preconceptions out the window. Along with my dignity.

"I know you came from a normal town," said Bethan. "It might take you a while to get the hang of things, but we're all willing to help you."

"I'm not from a coven," I blurted. "I'm—not. Whoever you think I am, you're wrong."

Way to go, Blair. Tell all your new colleagues they're wrong. Why not set the place on fire while you're at it?

I ignored the sarcastic voice in my head and put on a contrite expression. "What I meant to say is, I think you might have been misinformed."

19

"I assumed Alissa told you," Bethan said, her brow creasing. "She's the granddaughter of Madame Grey—*the* Madame Grey. So I assumed when she picked you, you were from a coven, too. Not a normal town."

"What's a not normal town?" Well, this place was a start.

"Most paranormals live in towns like this one," said Lizzie. "That's where we get most of our clients from. They can't advertise on the regular job market without attracting normals, and we don't let normals into this world."

Er, yeah. I think you just let the normal-est normal to ever normal into your office. They couldn't often get outsiders in if they'd sent Security McHottie to assess me in person, could they?

"If you were normal, you'd have been turned around by the wards," added Bethan. "Even buses can't come near here without breaking down. The town's magical shield stops anyone getting inside unless they're one of us."

I took a step backwards, shaking my head. "Magical shield? Seriously?"

"You're wearing one yourself," Bethan commented. "Hmm. Do buses often break down around you? That'd be why. I haven't been to a normal town or city, but I've heard our magical shields have similar effects on technology, too."

Wait. My disastrous driving lesson attempts. The fact that I couldn't stay on a bus or train longer than thirty minutes without it giving up the ghost...

No. Attempting to rationalise her words was an attempt to wring order from chaos, like trying to find a pocket of quiet at a loud house party. I'd know if I was like them... if I was magical.

"Most of us find it hard to live amongst humans," Bethan added. "There are other side effects even before we come into our powers. Technology breaks down around witches. Werewolves fly off the handle at the full moon. Fairies can't spend a long time around a lot of metal without sneezing violently."

Uneasily, I remembered that disastrous kitchen job. Silverware. No way. I wasn't going to lose my mind. I was a sane, normal, human, and as soon as I found someone who spoke sense, I'd be out of here faster than I could blink.

Croak. "Nobody said she didn't know… anything," rasped Blythe, who'd apparently got her voice back. "Look at her. She wants to leave."

Yes. She does. Wait—was she *reading my mind?*

"Blythe," Bethan said. "Kindly stop talking."

"Maybe if she doesn't end up with a dead body, she'll last longer than the last one," said Blythe.

There was a sharp intake of breath from Lizzie, while Bethan glared daggers at her. I dropped my gaze and spotted the rolled-up newspaper on the desk.

The photo on the cover was of the man who'd appeared in my head for a brief instant when I'd looked at the file in the desk drawer. Mr Bayer. The murder victim… and previous client.

The reason Bethan hadn't wanted me to look at the file was because the last client who'd spoken to my predecessor was *dead.* Murdered, actually. Two days before I got the call inviting me here.

3

Weirdly, it was murder that was the final straw. Not the werewolves or wands or witchery, or even the fact that everyone here seemed to think they knew who I was. I stared at the paper in horror. "Someone died *here*."

Bethan leaned over to me. "I'm sorry. It's unfortunate timing. Here, serious crimes are extremely rare."

I swallowed and looked closer at the rolled-up paper. It said the master spellmaker had been poisoned in his own place of employment.

"Your predecessor left because she was disturbed by the timing, but she was in no danger," added Bethan. "Nor are you. I promise."

"Told you she couldn't handle it," said Blythe.

I backed towards the door. Whatever Blythe's problem was with me, I didn't know or care. Maybe they were a murderous cult, maybe they were barking mad... maybe they meant every word, magic was real, and my Hogwarts letter had been returned for a refund. But one thing was absolutely clear—this place was dangerous. Sentient office printers weren't even the half of it.

I fled the office into the reception area. Callie wasn't there this time. I was penniless and more or less stranded, most of my possessions were with my questionable new flat-mate, and despite being stark raving bonkers, these people seemed to *know* me. Who the hell wouldn't want some answers at this point?

I sank to the floor, my hands over my face. Whether this place was truly dangerous or not, I hadn't thought so when I'd walked past the pretty houses and the lake which didn't exist on any map. Fairy Falls. Maybe I'd been under a spell since the moment I'd entered the village.

The door opened and Security McHottie walked in, because the universe had decided not to give me a break. I should also probably get his real name from someone at some point.

He looked at me. "What are you doing down there? Are you okay?"

"Sure, why not add murder to the list."

"List?" he echoed.

"Monster hunters, werewolves, witches, sentient printers and flying papers. And the *name*. Fairy Falls. This is… a circus."

"You found out about the murder?" He grimaced. "Sorry. It was last week, so the town's still a little on edge."

I shook my head. "It's not even that. I'm… normal. I was raised normal. I can't believe I'm even having this conversation."

His brows shot up. "Wait. You're a normal? You? Is that why…"

"Why I'm not supposed to be here, and why this is all like some weird acid trip? Yep."

ELLE ADAMS

"Oh no." He looked accusingly past the reception desk at a door near the back. "She didn't tell me. I wouldn't have interrogated you if I'd known you were a normal."

"Honestly, where I came from, *I* was considered eccentric." And why couldn't I shut my stupid mouth? It wasn't like me to spill my feelings in an ugly mess in front of an attractive stranger. Okay, except when wine was involved. "And now everyone is participating in a shared delusion to make me completely lose my mind. Too bad. I figured out your game first."

His brow furrowed. "Do you think I'd waste my time hoaxing a stranger? It's forbidden, for a start. Don't mess with the normals. But I don't think you are one. This is all empty space as far as the humans are concerned. They walk right past us."

"Witches," I said. "Witches, werewolves… vampires? Zombies?"

"All the above, and more. Sorry for assuming you were in the know. That can't have helped."

I rested my head on my knees. "Please tell me I'm dreaming."

"You're not dreaming. Do you normally dream about magic?" He sounded genuinely curious.

"Usually I dream about missing the bus or showing up at work in my underwear."

Well done, Blair. He already thought me a fool. I couldn't sink any lower in his estimation.

"I suspect that's because your powers were suppressed, living amongst normals. This town is a magical hot spot."

"You're all completely mad." I raised my eyes to the ceiling. "I'm sorry. You're nice and everything, but you're all…"

"Magical? It's real. I should tell the boss you didn't know. I'm surprised. She's usually efficient at checking her potential candidates' details before calling."

"Apparently I have an identical twin."

"I'm fairly sure there's only one Blair." He chuckled a little. "I never did introduce myself properly, did I? I'm Nathan."

"You're a witch as well? No, you said you… hunt monsters. Do I fall into that category?"

"No. Hunters deal with paranormal rogues. Fairies hiding amongst humans, werewolves without a clan, that type of thing. But I don't do that anymore."

"Paranormal rogues." I snort-laughed, attractively. "Sure. Why not."

"Why not indeed? Have you ever had reason to suspect you're more than human?"

"More than human?" I spoke to my knees. "Nope. I like Harry Potter books as much as the next person, but I'm pretty sure the owl carrying my Hogwarts letter flew into a lamp post en route."

He laughed. Did he find me amusing? Hot guys didn't laugh at my terrible jokes. They also didn't listen while I spilt my sob story all over the floor and then sat in a puddle of my own failures.

"I don't belong here," I told him. "Plainly, someone hired the wrong person. Maybe someone who has the same name as me. It's plausible."

Less plausible was the fact that every single detail on the profile the boss had found matched mine exactly, unless someone had uploaded my details to a paranormal recruitment site as a prank. But that seemed fairly pointless if they knew I wasn't magical.

He shook his head. "No, it was definitely you she meant to hire."

"How'd they find me?"

"You'll have to ask your boss that. I don't know. But it's rare that one of us grows up entirely unaware of this world."

"I'm an orphan," I said, my voice brittle. "I was raised in foster care, and I wouldn't know if my family was magical because they've never got in touch with me."

He took a step towards me as though uncertain whether to comfort me or not. "I'm sorry that happened to you, but you're amongst equals now. You wouldn't have known what you are if nobody told you. As I said—there are rules affecting how much normals are allowed to know about us."

"You all sound so logical." I climbed to my feet. "Why does it make so much sense?"

In the fantasy books I read, 'you're a wizard' came with a big fanfare and huge revelation. It didn't strike me as the type of thing you blundered into by accident.

He glanced over his shoulder. "The boss will talk you through everything, if you decide to stay. There won't be any more unwelcome surprises."

"I think I've used up my lifetime quota of surprises," I said. "So you work for her, too?"

"I'm the town's security. I work for whoever hires me. It's rare that we get visitors at all, so they wanted someone to check on you. Speak of the devil…"

Another door had opened, and a woman with long silver-white hair strode out. "Is the new girl here?"

Nathan gave me a look clearly indicating that he wouldn't stop me from leaving. But I dearly wanted to know who it was who'd found my details floating around in the void of graduate job application websites and somehow plucked out that I was… not-normal from that.

Okay. Let's meet the boss. I'm sure there's a rational explanation.

The boss—Veronica—beckoned me into an office, pulling out a chair. A plush chair. Everything was plush, and fluffy, a total contrast with her sharp professional business suit. Smiling kittens looked down at me from the walls. I stared in disbelief. Fluffy kittens should not look so creepy.

"Overkill?" she asked, then snapped her fingers. The walls emptied themselves of fluffy kittens and turned to beige instead, while the chair became oak wood. Now it looked more like a headteacher's office. An improvement, though not much.

"I have to apologise," she said. "It's no way to start a new job."

I sunk in my seat. "I think you have the wrong person."

"No, we have the right person. It was presumptuous of me to assume that you'd be fully aware of your magical status despite having spent most of your life in an entirely normal environment. You must have a lot of questions."

"How did you find me?" I asked. "I know—my details showed up online. I don't remember uploading a profile on that site, though."

"We scan the normal sites, too," she said. "I have a gift for picking out the best candidates. Bethan gets it from me—my daughter," she added in explanation. "I hired her for her skills, though, not because we're related."

Uh-huh. Some things apparently didn't change whether you were a normal or not.

"Anyway," she went on, "since we already have the local covens represented, I decided to reach out to you. We specialise in dealing with paranormal clients who often have trouble tracking down potential employees. Because all magical towns are hidden as well as this one, and the normals' world blocks all magic from view. I assume you've never experienced anything weird before."

I nearly laughed. "Aside from coming here? No."

But that wasn't true. What Bethan had said rang too many familiar notes. I'd never felt like I fit into the everyday world, and was perpetually one step behind everyone else. I moved between jobs, between houses, like I was following an itch I couldn't scratch. I assumed it was down to being the only one of my friends who hadn't settled down, but now I had to wonder if there was more to it than that.

"If you're new to magic, you'll need a tutor," said Veronica. "Madame Grey will sort you out. She leads the Meadowsweet Coven... she owns the whole town, technically. But you won't need to use those skills for this job. Your profile said you've worked in recruitment before."

"I have. But I was under the impression I'd be sending emails and making phone calls. I thought technology didn't work around magic."

"Normal technology doesn't," she said. "Ours is special. Lizzie's coven specialises in magical technology. We live in the modern world, don't we? Most of us didn't grow up totally isolated."

Point taken. "And the man who died?"

"I'm sure they'll catch the killer in no time. It's unfortunate that you had to move here so soon after. But it'll be solved. Put it out of mind, if you can. I think you've had enough information to absorb."

No kidding. "Wait—what about my family? I'm adopted. There are no records. At least, I've never been able to find them. So were they witches, too?"

"You can ask Madame Grey," she said. "She knows all the covens, local or not."

Might my family still be alive? Stop there—that was too far. I needed to get my thoughts under control before I ran screaming from a situation that was frankly more fascinating than anything I'd ever encountered in my life.

"We can help you learn everything you need to, and you already have accommodation sorted," said Veronica. "So... want to give it a go?"

My mouth hung open. I *should* say no. But I'd been

offered a lifeline, and aside from Blythe, the others seemed genuinely fun to work with. It wasn't like I was inexperienced in this particular job field. I just needed to stick the word 'paranormal' in front of everything and try not to make too many Hogwarts references.

"All right," I found myself saying. "I'll give it a try."

4

———

I gripped the phone as though if I held on tightly enough, it'd stop me from dissolving into another meltdown.

Bethan's presence at my side wasn't helping matters. She was a human whirlwind perched on a rotating office chair. The sound of shuffling papers and tapping keys permeated the background as I struggled to get my head back into Office Phone Call Mode. At least all the noise convinced me I hadn't imagined the situation. Let's face it: nobody would get this many people involved in creating such a ridiculous setup to mess with me. And despite the pinch marks on my arms, I still hadn't woken up yet. It was real. All of it.

The sound of a dial tone continued. I was told to keep trying until I got hold of the potential candidate.

"Hello?" I asked, as someone finally picked up. "Is this Mr Vaughn Llewellyn?"

Grr.

A wolf. The image was clear and insistent this time, infiltrating my mind and making me completely forget my line.

Nope. I need to take in the whole witch thing before I can start having more wolf hallucinations.

"Hello, this is… Dritch & Co recruitment agency. We've found your profile and we believe you'd be a prime candidate for this position. We'd like to invite you to an interview."

The growling resolved into a human-sounding voice. "Who did you say you were?"

"Eldritch & Co."

My brain heard his raspy voice and said *werewolf.* Nope. No wolves. Put the thought into a drawer and close it firmly.

There was a pause on the other end of the line. Oh. He'd said something when I'd been lost in thoughts of wolves. "Can you say that again?"

"I said, didn't you call me about another job last week?" he growled.

Wait. I looked down at the file with his name on it. I knew that name. I'd seen it recently… on the list of clients interviewed by Mr Bayer.

This man was one of the potential employees for the last client. One of the people rejected for the job before the client's untimely death.

"Is there a problem?" he asked, in his raspy voice.

"Nope. It's my first day here. The client would be interested in interviewing you if you're available…" I rattled off the rest of my speech, my mind in freefall. I was pretty sure his file didn't say he was a werewolf, but that was probably my brain's attempt to cope with a rapidly unravelling situation. But he'd been for an interview at Mr Bayer's place right before he'd died. And what about the other names on the call list?

When the call finished, I skimmed through today's list of candidates. Then I looked up, checked nobody was watching, and picked up the file for the previous employee. Werewolf dude wasn't the only name that matched. Mr Bayer had interviewed the potential candidates the same day he'd been murdered.

"You don't have to look at that," said Bethan, leaning across from her own desk.

"I know, but—look at these names." I held up the file. "The guy I just spoke to on the phone was interviewed by Mr Bayer the day he died."

Her eyes widened. "Are you sure?"

"Yeah, I think I'd remember the name 'Vaughn Llewellyn'. There are others here, too." I put the file back down. "How'd he die, anyway? A werewolf bite?" Oops. I hadn't meant to say the last part aloud.

"No. He was poisoned, the report says. What do you mean, a werewolf bite?"

"He was a werewolf, right? The guy I spoke to." *Stop talking.*

She took the file from me, momentarily pausing in her multitasking. "The file listed him as human. A wizard. How do you know he was a werewolf?"

"I just... do." Because apparently images of wolves were stalking me today. But if there was any place I could safely mention that without everyone thinking I'd lost my marbles, it was here. "When he spoke to me on the phone, I kept getting images of wolves. Might that be a magic thing? It's been happening since I came here. I... saw him, without actually seeing him. If that makes sense."

She frowned. "We can certainly look into his details, but he's not listed as a werewolf. Then again, I don't remember every client. Was he rejected for the position?"

"Must have been, if he's on my call list for today," I said.

Bethan glanced over at the papers on my desk. "This is our busiest season. I'm sorry for the mix-up. But if he *is* a werewolf, he's required by law to disclose it on his application form. Paranormal authorities' rules, not ours."

"And if he's breaking one rule, he might have broken others." Murder, though? Werewolf or not, Callie was one, too… *stop that.* I didn't have any business making snap judgements on strangers based on weird thoughts that came into my head. What I needed was to do my job.

"Is there a police office here?" I asked. "Do they have a copy of the same list?"

"There's a small one. Few staff. Paranormals generally police our own. The werewolves certainly do. But… hmm. Maybe this *is* evidence, and I don't think the police have it. We need the case cleared up as quickly as possible."

She was still looking at me like… well, like I'd told her she was a witch and everyone around me was either the same or some other type of paranormal creature. What I'd done couldn't be *that* unusual, right? Not that I was exactly an expert on the subject.

"I didn't mean to imply I don't believe you," she added. "No… I need to check something first."

She opened the desk drawer. I stared into what appeared to be a massive vault crammed with enough papers and files to fill an entire house. A cage sat at the back, emitting squeaking noises, and… "Is that a bookshelf?"

"Yep." She pulled a stick of wood wrapped in a silver ribbon from a container of other miscellaneous objects. A magic wand. I stared in fascination, then jumped as the office printer whirred to life when she pointed her wand at it. Then it spat a piece of paper at her, which she caught by her fingertips.

"You have to ask nicely," Lizzie said, barely looking up from her keyboard. She, and thankfully Blythe, had returned to work once it was clear I was staying, and Blythe hadn't made any more derogatory remarks.

ELLE ADAMS

Bethan flipped the paper over in one hand. "It doesn't like any of us except you. You know that."

Lizzie shrugged. "You never gave it a chance."

Bethan threw the paper down. "Okay... let's try this." She waved the wand, and a fire leapt up on the desk.

I wheeled the chair back so fast I nearly fell off it. "Oh... my god. The desk is on fire." Way to state the obvious, Blair. I braced myself for sprinklers and fire alarms, but nobody else even looked up from their desks.

"It's contained." Bethan held the paper over the simmering candle-sized fire. The flame leapt higher, devouring every inch of the page until nothing remained.

Bethan leaned over, brow furrowed, reading something in the flames that I couldn't see. The smell of burning cloves filled the room. Then she looked up at me.

"You're right." She waved a hand and the flames vanished. "He's a werewolf, all right."

"And... what does that make me?"

"Talented. Ask Alissa, and she'll find you a tutor right away. I get the feeling you'll need it."

Yeah. Maybe I will. Now my curiosity couldn't be tamed. I could tell if someone was paranormal without looking at them?

"Is that normal, for a witch?" I asked.

"Normal? No such thing here," she said breezily. "Your powers must have been dormant for your whole life. I've never met anyone else in your position, but it's definitely unique—not in a bad way. You haven't done anything wrong. You might just have helped us, actually."

I rested my head against the back of the desk chair. "Maybe. Is it a common talent, though?"

"No, but it depends on your bloodline. That determines the nature of your dominant gift."

Blythe made another dismissive noise. Mind-reading

34

must be her gift. Veronica had implied Bethan's had to do with being able to track people down... or possibly do the jobs of twelve people at the same time. Lizzie could make sentient printers. And me?

"Wow," I said. "To think I thought I'd be answering phone calls, not accidentally identifying murderers."

Maybe I'd gone too far. But she laughed. None of them seemed bothered that at some point in my fourth call centre job, I'd completely lost the ability to switch on an effective filter at work and not return the customers' rudeness with the sarcastic response it deserved.

"What about the werewolf, then?" I asked. "Do we send the police in? Or—" I nearly said *monster hunter security guards,* but held my tongue.

"Not yet. I'll ask Callie to speak to the leader of the local pack and see if there are any possible strays."

"Wait," I said. "I mean—what if he's the killer? It seems a pretty big thing to lie about. He's supposed to be coming in for an interview tomorrow anyway... maybe I can slide in some probing questions concerning his last interview. I might be able to pick up anything else from him in person, too. I mean, if I can tell someone's a werewolf over the phone..."

She nodded slowly. "Good thinking. I'll tell Callie and the boss in case he *is* dangerous, but I'll ask them not to spread it around. There are a dozen innocent reasons someone might hide their identity. If you're sure."

No, I wasn't sure. What in the world was I doing? I needed to settle down before trying to catch rogue were-wolves. *Maybe that's a job for the resident retired monster hunter.*

"You look a little tired. Want me to get you a coffee? We have a special brand for motivation. Not that caffeine isn't motivational enough on its own."

"Motivational coffee?" I raised an eyebrow. "Sure, why not."

She walked to a machine in the corner, all shiny black chrome and covered in buttons. Her wand appeared in her hand, and she tapped the button with a picture of a coffee cup on it. Immediately, two coffees appeared on the desk.

"Wow." I walked around the machine, but I couldn't see where the coffee had been conjured up from. Attempting to figure out magic would probably just give me a headache.

"Perks of the job—we each get one motivational coffee a day. Any more tends to have adverse side effects."

"Do I even want to ask?" I took the coffee and sipped it. It had an odd aftertaste, weirdly sweet.

"Luck is worse," she said. "You get one day of life being perfect and then every client flakes on you for the rest of the week."

"Fun." I took another sip. A jolt of optimism straightened shoulders I hadn't realised were slouching and banished every scrap of doubt from my mind. "Wow. I should have started the day with this."

The voice telling me to run for the hills had already been growing quieter by the second. But I couldn't leave now, could I? Someone was dead. And somehow, I knew one of the potential killers was hiding a secret. "Do you have background info on the other interviewees, too?" I asked Bethan. "There are a couple more names on the call list for today which match the ones who were interviewed to work for Mr Bayer. Unless it's too much of a risk?"

"Not at all. You have an ironclad excuse, and the police are the arrest-first-ask-questions-later sort. Veronica put enough defensive spells on the building that nobody will be able to harm you in here."

"Excellent." I loaded up my computer, which thankfully seemed to work more or less the same as a standard one, aside from the weird vampire logo and a couple of odd additions to the keyboard that looked suspiciously like arcane symbols.

"Are you slacking off over there?" Blythe asked. I instinctively moved the files to cover the incriminating one.

"No, I'm giving her some pointers," said Bethan. "She's new, and you can't expect her to know everything right away."

Blythe gave me a piercing look and I resisted the impulse to shrink back. They'd clearly had some kind of dispute before I'd arrived. Maybe to do with hiring an outsider, or hiring someone new so soon after their last colleague had been terrified into running. Whatever the reason, I had zero patience for her attitude. "Is there a problem?"

"You have some nerve barging into an active police investigation when you haven't even been here a day."

So she'd been eavesdropping. "I'm not barging in anywhere."

"You can't pull that one on me. I can read thoughts." She smiled. "You found out how specialist talents work, right? That's mine."

Great. No privacy from someone who hated my guts for no apparent reason. Though I couldn't think what thoughts she'd picked up on that might have caused her to hate me on sight. I'd met my fair share of petty bullies in my life. They said 'they'll grow out of it', but that was a lie. Petty bullies at school grew up to be petty bullying adults and passed on the same habits to their children. If you ignored them, they decided they were more entitled to act like they had a licence to treat people like dirt. Best to confront them head-on.

"And I know what you think *yours* is," she added. "I wouldn't get involved in werewolf pack business."

"I'm not getting involved in anything," I said. "I'd just like to know if the candidates I'm speaking to on the phone are criminals or not before I get them a job."

"Maybe I'll call the police myself," she said. "Steve will set them right."

That shouldn't have sounded as threatening as it did. They couldn't arrest me as an outsider, could they?

"The candidate might be innocent," said Bethan. "I'm still pulling together the information, besides. Blythe, you're outnumbered. Go back to work."

She hissed out a breath. "You're clueless, aren't you?" she said to me.

"I'm learning. And Bethan is capable of making her own decisions. I didn't tell her to help me."

Blythe said in acid tones, "She doesn't even belong here. She's a fairy, not a witch."

"Excuse me?"

"What I said." Her eyes narrowed. "Pity the boss has yet to find out you're here to destabilise the balance."

"I have no idea what you're talking about."

There was a flash from behind the computer, and Blythe ducked her head. "Don't you think about zapping me again," she said to Lizzie.

"Then get back to work," Lizzie retaliated.

Blythe rolled her eyes, but got the message and thankfully returned her attention to her own client list.

"Don't pay her any attention," said Bethan.

"Was she right?" I said, more confused than ever. "I thought—you said I was a witch."

"Your file did," she said. "I have no idea where she picked that up."

"Not from my thoughts, that's for sure." My mind whirled. The motivational coffee had worn off pretty fast. I was well and truly exhausted. And if I apparently had to go to meet the leading witch later, I might need a power nap first.

Or a ticket home. To my not-home.

No. I'm not going back there. Witch… fairy… I could be the Loch Ness Monster and I still wouldn't want to go back to my old life, not now I'd experienced this. Whatever came next depended on how I handled myself at Dritch—*Eldritch* —and Co.

5

As my first day drew to a close, it was time to go and meet my flatmate. The good news: I wasn't living with a lunatic or cultist. The bad news: there would be no taking a break from the madness, because my next task was to introduce myself to the local coven leader and hope I wouldn't be ousted as an impostor and tossed into the lake.

It sounded like this Meadowsweet Coven—along with its leader—was highly influential. Hot Security Guy—Nathan— had said this Madame Grey person owned the whole town. At least I thought he did. Our whole conversation seemed like an embarrassing hallucination from the same place as my showing-up-for-work-in-my-underwear dream collection.

While I had the address to my new flat from the email I'd saved to my phone before my internet connection had cut out, it seemed to point to an old manor house on the corner of one cobbled street, way too fancy for the price range I'd been given. I kept walking, but found no modern-looking apartment blocks. They'd look out of place here. Even the air smelled different. Cleaner. I knew why. I hadn't seen a single car here, or bus. Did they all ride broomsticks or magic carpets? I hadn't seen any of those either, but the town was bigger than it'd seemed from the map, and they must get around somehow.

My phone signal had come back, but seemed to be hooked up to a line called Paramobile, and none of the messages I tried to send to my friends at home went through. They did have working computers here, so maybe there was a special Wi-Fi for paranormals, too. I hoped so, because I needed a hint that the world outside still existed.

"Hey, Blair," said Alissa, opening the door of the manor house from the inside as I walked past it for the fourth time. "Thought I recognised you standing out there."

"I did get the right house?" I looked up at the balconied windows. "Wow."

"We only have half the bottom floor," she said. "I brought your suitcase in. You have the window facing the garden, but we can swap if you'd prefer. We also have a kobold—house cleaner. He comes once a week. Otherwise, it's just us. Sounds good?"

Better than good. "I didn't think... I expected a tower block or something."

"We're not quite that modern here," she said. "We make do with what we have."

Make do? I could have fitted my old house in here three times over, and there'd been six people living in it.

"No, I love it," I said honestly. "I used to live in a house of teenage undergraduates who never did the dishes and hung dirty underwear out the window. Anything else is paradise."

She smiled. "I've lived here all my life, but I've always wanted to go to a human city or town. I'm looking forward to hearing all about it later."

Hmm. I have my doubts it'll be as fun as you think.

41

The interior of the house was even more spectacular. High ceilings, wooden floors so polished that I could see our reflections in them, and a carved staircase at the end.

Alissa pushed open a door on the right, revealing a wide living room. I'd have said the place belonged to a fussy old lady, witch or not. Velvet drapes framed the wide, arched windows. A fluffy black cat lay sleeping on the sofa. All the furniture was made of dark wood, old and expensive-looking.

True to her word, Alissa had moved my suitcase into my new bedroom. It was three times the size of my last one, with oak furniture and wide windows open onto the lush green garden. I gaped at it for a few seconds. "Oh, wow."

At my last place, the doors frequently fell off the cupboards, the heating broke every winter, and almost everything had questionable stains and signs of wear and tear. I backed out of the bedroom, my gaze drinking in every unnoticed inch of the living room—the ornate fireplace, the surprisingly modern kitchenette at the side, the plush chairs which somehow didn't have cat hair on them despite their fluffy occupant.

Witchcraft. It was the only explanation.

"I should be paying ten times the rent on this place," I said, shaking my head.

"Don't tell the landlord." She winked. "Madame Grey is my grandmother. She's the leader of the Meadowsweet Coven and owns half a dozen properties in the town, including this one."

"The Meadowsweet Coven? I've heard that name before."

"It's my coven," she said. "Since its members founded the town, they own most of it. Or rather, my grandmother does. She's offered to meet with you at the witches' main head-quarters in an hour, to help you figure out which type of dominant magic you have. Then you choose how to proceed from there."

"What, you mean learn magic?" My inner thirteen-year-old vibrated with excitement. While any kind of magic would be awesome, my first step would be to figure out how to cast that frog spell on Blythe.

"You can sign up to evening classes," she said. "If you want actual qualifications in witchcraft, it'll take a little longer. Each witch or wizard has a natural proficiency in a certain area, but almost anything can be done with a few props."

If I took on extra classes on top of full-time work, I'd have my hands full. But I had the distinct impression it wouldn't be anything like school. And I hadn't moved to a paranormal town only to end up doing the same boring job I did in NormalsVille. *Magic. Yes, please.*

"Bethan implied there were a few covens here," I said. "You all seem to know one another pretty well."

"Madame Grey knows everyone," said Alissa. "As for the rest of us, some covens are larger than others. Anyone can join a coven, but there are usually conditions to entry. But I think that's probably too much information for you to absorb right now."

"Honestly, the part I'm having the most trouble with is the idea of *me* being magical," I admitted. "I've been told I couldn't have known since I spent my whole life living with normal humans—but you'd think someone would have noticed."

"Not if you didn't know your family. Bethan told me about that, too. I'm sorry." Her eyes shone with sympathy.

I'd had that a lot. At school, anyway. Everyone knew I was the adopted kid. But knowing what I did now, my old life looked different through the lens that had slid into place in the last few hours. As though I was looking at someone else's history. A stranger's.

"No worries." I cracked a smile. "Guess I'll get to be as surprised as everyone else when you find out what my talent is."

"Yeah. Madame Grey's doubtless looking into it," she said. "I'm—to be honest, I'm intrigued to know which bloodline you came from. It didn't show up on your file."

"Which is why I was so weirded out that my boss knew I was a witch."

"She probably used a spell to find you."

Like the divining spell they used to find out that guy was a werewolf. Which I'd been able to tell just from hearing his voice. What would this Madame Grey make of that?

"What do you think of Veronica, anyway? I've heard she's eccentric."

"She seems nice. Her office is a little strange, though."

"I heard she changed her surname to 'Eldritch' on a whim after a divorce, but nobody really knows the details there. She's a daughter of nomads who met on a paranormal cruise ship—an English witch and an Irish shifter. She mostly got the witch genes and passed those on to Bethan."

"Is that how it works? Magic is passed on through bloodlines?"

"Generally it is. Even in cases like yours, your real parents were almost certainly magical. Anyway, I'll give you some peace to unpack. We can explore the town afterwards if the session finishes early. I'm not sure how much she wants to go through with you on your first day."

"Sure." I laid my suitcase down on its side. Was there any point in unpacking if I might have to grab my bags and leave at any moment? I hadn't even arranged for the rest of my possessions to be moved here, since the whole thing had happened in such a hurry. I'd been intending to call a moving company, but I somehow doubted the phone signal situation extended to normal towns.

I sank onto the bed. What a day. And it wasn't even over yet.

I was too wired to nap, so I changed from my work clothes into a fresh outfit. I had no idea what I was expected to wear. This Madame Grey seemed to be highly respected, and I doubted jeans would cut it. I settled for a longish skirt and my fanciest top—*not* the one I'd worn on my ill-advised wine-fuelled night out on Saturday. How had that only been two days ago?

I hung my work clothes within easy reach, checked my phone again, and sent another text message to Rebecca. *Message failed.* I thought so. Did the witches here have delivery companies? I supposed I could buy crockery from town, and the room was already furnished at least. And then there was the garden. I'd bounced between locations so much that I never stayed anywhere long enough for it to look like home, but I'd never had a proper garden before. Let alone one with extensive grounds and strange, exotic-looking plants.

I found Alissa on the sofa in the living room, stroking the black cat. It looked up warily at the sight of me.

"Hey," she said. "This is Roald. He's my familiar."

At this point I didn't even blink. "Hey, Roald."

I expected him to answer, but he merely licked a paw and went back to enjoying being stroked. "I thought familiars talked."

"Not exactly, but we intuitively understand one another," she said. "Not all witches have familiars... they're usually introduced at school, but it's a relatively recent practice. I think you have enough to cope with at the moment, but let me know if you'd like to check with the coven."

"Maybe see if I *am* a witch first."

She rose to her feet. "Of course you are, silly. No normal

could have come this far. Sounds like you did a stellar job of coping on your first day at the office, too."

Aside from the sitting-on-the-floor incident. "So what do you do?" I asked. "I mean, work-wise?"

"I work at the hospital," she said. "My speciality is healing magic. The hospital's at the end of the high street, so if you need me to get anything for you while you're at work, just let me know. I couldn't help noticing you only brought one suitcase."

"Yeah, I didn't have the chance to arrange to have my other stuff moved here," I said. "But normals can't find the place."

"Right," she said. "I'll ask Madame Grey."

Her again. It sounded like this woman had the authority to declare whether or not I was really a witch. My nerves spiked.

"Something wrong?" she asked.

"I found out about Mr Bayer," I admitted. "It weirded me out a little."

"Oh," said Alissa. "It's rare for something like that to happen here. How did you find out? The others were supposed to keep quiet."

"I saw a newspaper lying around," I said, throwing caution to the winds. Alissa seemed friendly enough—almost too much so, for someone I'd never met before. But it didn't sound like the residents of this town had many opportunities to meet new people, especially normals like me. "Also, when I was calling up potential candidates for another client, I didn't realise that one of the people on the list was already rejected for that same job. Several others were the same. Do the police know?"

She blinked. "I have no idea. The police presumably have a suspect list, but the gargoyles never let anyone interfere with their jobs. They're efficient, but scary."

"The police are gargoyles." Of course they were. Even the most innocuous questions came with bizarre answers as far as Fairy Falls went.

"I keep forgetting how little you know," she said. "Sorry, that sounds patronising. I actually thought about going into teaching, so I might be able to give you some pointers. There aren't many opportunities to help people learn magic, since we're mostly born into it."

"So children go to magic school?"

"Yes. Madame Grey tried to push me into teaching instead of nursing, but you don't know real fear until you've been cornered by a five-year-old wielding a fully activated wand. Luckily, patients aren't allowed to bring them into the hospital. Much less hazardous."

"Wow." I shook my head. "Aside from witches, who else is there? I've met one werewolf…" Possibly two.

"Oh, Callie," she said. "She's the werewolf chief's beloved daughter. They watch over one another pretty closely. Can't have wolves running too close to human territory."

"I guess that's where security comes in?"

"Oh." Her eyes gleamed. "Nathan met you at the gates, right? I thought I heard some of the other witches grumbling. He's never given any of them the time of day."

So I'd made a complete fool of myself in front of the hottest guy in town. Awesome. "Aren't they scared because he's an ex-monster hunter?"

"It's the dangerous vibe they like," she said. "I take it you're single? I assume you are, since you haven't been frantically trying to call anyone."

"There's no signal. But you're right. Been there, done that. Why?"

"Because certain individuals are notorious gossips."

Like Blythe. Who hated me, for reasons unknown. "Honestly, I'm still trying to get the hang of this place. Romance is the last thing on my mind."

"Understandable. We should probably leave soon, if you're ready. Madame Grey doesn't like lateness."

That didn't come as any surprise. I fetched my coat and took in deep breaths to calm my nerves. "If I'm a witch, do I get a wand? I saw Bethan use a divining spell earlier and she nearly set the desk on fire."

"You won't be doing that for a while. They don't give out wands until you prove you're ready for the basics."

Probably for the best, considering household objects were a hazard to me on a good day.

We left the house, and again, I had to marvel at the absence of traffic. It hadn't got dark outside yet, but it probably would by the time we got out of the meeting. I assumed it wouldn't last all night, but it wasn't like I had a handbook or brochure. *Witching for Dummies* would be handy right now.

Alissa took the lead. "By the way, it probably goes without saying, but if there's anything you want to ask me about magic, I'd be happy to answer."

"Sure."

The witches' main headquarters was a pleasant-looking house around the same size as my new home. Curtains of ivy trailed down the brick walls, and the pungent smell of unfamiliar flowers hung around the front garden.

Alissa halted outside. "This is the witches' main gathering spot. Madame Grey owns it, but she doesn't live here."

"Is there anything she doesn't own?" I couldn't help asking.

"Anything marked as non-witch territory," she said. "Probably shouldn't ask her that, though. I don't need to tell you to watch what you say to her."

Translation: if I knew best, I shouldn't say anything at all.

"She'll be kind to you, as you're a newbie," she added. "Best get inside."

The doors creaked loudly, announcing our entrance. A wide hall branched off into several rooms, one of which was filled with a group of strangers sitting in chairs before a tall woman dressed in grey. Madame Grey, I'd guess. Her grey hair was combed back, a large number of earrings dangled from her ears, and a faint silver sheen shone from the wand in her right hand.

Despite our being several minutes early, the way heads turned in our direction reminded me of showing up late for class. Alissa hadn't mentioned there'd be other witches here.

Madame Grey nodded to Alissa. "There you are. And this must be the new girl, Blair."

I gave an awkward wave. "Hi. I'm Blair." Obviously. Because she just said my name.

"Hi, Blair," chorused a dozen voices.

Nobody was this friendly. Correction: nobody who hadn't been ordered to be nice to the newbie was this friendly. Some of their smiles were strained, or overly curious-looking. The setup looked more like a sermon than a magic lesson. *Or a trial.* Had they come to see if she planned to kick me out?

"Take a seat," Madame Grey said, a touch impatiently. "From what my granddaughter tells me, you're new to everything. Why not tell everyone a little about yourself?"

Maybe I should have written a speech. "There's not much to say. I didn't know I was a witch until I moved here. I lived… in a normal town. With normals." Now the *word* 'normal' didn't sound remotely, well, normal to me. "I didn't know anything about all this until today."

"Oh, you poor thing," said an older witch.

"You don't believe that, do you?" another loudly whispered. "Someone test her."

I was used to being treated like I was half my age. It was a little better than being yelled at, but irritation prickled at me. "I couldn't have come in here if I was a normal," I said. "So clearly there's something up."

"Which coven?" asked another of the witches. "She can't be from the Moonbeams, they'd never go near a normal town."

Alissa stepped in. "We're not sure yet. We were hoping to find out."

"I was adopted," I added. "I don't know my birth parents' details. My foster parents said they lived in London." A big city didn't seem a great place for a witch to live, especially given the effect we had on public transport.

"There's a simpler way." Madame Grey pointed at a redheaded witch who wore so many bangles that she resembled a human Christmas tree. "Rita is best at divining spells. She'll divine what type of magic is your predominant type."

All eyes swivelled to face us.

"Stop gawking," Rita snapped at the others. "I'll need some privacy to figure it out. She's an odd one."

Just what I needed to hear in front of a roomful of witches.

Alissa leaned to whisper in my ear. "Go with her. She's safe."

Let's clear this up, then.

Rita beckoned me out of the room and through the adjacent door. Eager to get away from the others' stares, I followed her. Curiosity about my family warred with the instinct to run, but the witch turned and gave me a smile, accompanied by the jangling noise of the bands up both her arms. "Overbearing, isn't she?"

The room contained a number of tables and chairs, like a classroom. She waved her wand—which was decorated with several red bands—and a fire leapt into being on the desk. Even after seeing Bethan do the same earlier, I still jumped.

"Divining isn't the most accurate form of magic," she admitted, striding over to the leaping flames. "Especially with little to go by." She conjured up a piece of paper and tossed it into the fire—I glimpsed an image of my own face before the flames devoured it. "But this will tell me your basic magic type. It *should* do, anyway. But it's not showing…" She looked up, confusion flashing across her features. "Hmm."

"What is it?"

She waved the wand, the flames vanished, and Madame Grey opened the door. "What's the verdict?"

"Hang on," said Rita. "Let's try this again."

She conjured another piece of paper and tossed it into the flames. You'd think there'd be a more environmentally friendly way of practising witchcraft considering how otherwise modern things were here.

Madame Grey moved closer to Rita, and they exchanged whispers.

"What is it?" I asked. "What—I'm not a witch, am I? I'm not paranormal at all. This was all a mistake." I'd never felt so much like a deflating balloon, and today's events had some pretty strong competition.

"No, you're paranormal all right," she said. "But the test is saying you're a fairy."

Blythe. Her smug face flashed before my eyes and I sat down slowly in the nearest seat. "I—I'm a fairy?"

Madame Grey looked at me, her expression unreadable. "That's what the test says."

Rita cleared her throat. "I don't quite understand… I'm

going to have to look at your profile again. Because my detection spells are rarely wrong."

I'd know if I was a fairy. But wouldn't I have known I was a witch, too? "Does that mean I have no magic at all?"

"No, certainly not," said Madame Grey. "Fairies are close enough to humans that we share some similarities."

"Are there other fairies here?" I got to my feet. "In that case, it's them I should be meeting with."

"No," said Madame Grey, looking me up and down. "There are no fairy representatives, and as leader of the town's council, I'm still in charge of dealing with newcomers. I'll have to look into your history. The more time you spend around magic, the more it'll adapt to you. If you leave… you'll face difficulties, in the normal world. But if you still want to do that, then just give me the word."

She's offering me a way out. "No. I *used* magic. I can tell what type of paranormal someone is just by hearing their voice. Is there a way for me to learn what that means?"

"Perhaps," she mused. "I'll discuss it with the rest of the council."

Oh no. The whole reason I'd been hired in the first place was because Veronica thought I was a witch. Would I even be allowed to stay after that? Would I upset the balance? Why was I even having thoughts like that? That was Blythe's line, and she was probably talking nonsense.

She'd known I was a fairy.

Murders, unintentional deception and gossiping witches aside, the idea of walking away was about as appealing as skinny-dipping in the lake. I needed answers—concrete ones —about how I'd ended up living with humans to begin with.

"Come back and talk to me at the same time tomorrow if you intend to stay," Madame Grey said. "There won't be a coven meeting this time… there isn't supposed to be one today, but everyone wanted a look at the new witch."

What a first impression they'd had. "I guess I won't be able to learn magic, then. Can you teach fairies?"

She gave me an imperious look. "I've yet to find a student I was unable to teach."

And she swept from the room, hopefully to tell the other witches to stop gossiping about me and head home. The last thing I wanted to see was Blythe's smugness that she'd apparently got it right when she'd guessed I wasn't a witch. It must have been a guess. Reading my thoughts wouldn't have helped, right? After all, I hadn't known a thing.

"Don't worry," Rita said. "We'll get to the bottom of this."

"Thanks anyway," I said, taking her words as an invitation to duck out of the room.

Apparently, Madame Grey had dismissed the congregation or they'd left of their own accord. Only Alissa remained, waiting for me.

"She told you?" I asked. "If you don't want me sharing your flat any longer, I can find somewhere else." If I ever got an internet connection, anyway.

"No, I don't mind at all," she said. "If you were a werewolf, it might be a different story. But I'm trusting you won't turn into a wolf in your sleep."

How could she be this casual? "Might there have been a mistake?"

"Maybe. But we won't throw you out over a little thing like that. Fairies are rare here, but not in the paranormal world. You're fine."

Except my boss might not see it that way. She was the one who'd found my profile and somehow used that to work out I was a witch. I didn't want to be the one to tell her she was wrong. Maybe my ability was a fairy one, not a witch one. It must be.

"I honestly don't know," she said, when I asked her. "Fairies tend to keep to themselves, so we're not experts on their magic. I'm sure my grandmother will come up with a plan of action to learn what your abilities are. Want to get something to eat on the way back?"

"That'd be great. Thanks." I dug my hands in my pockets and kept walking. "Does nobody drive here at all?" The aura of calm over the town persisted with the absence of traffic noise humming in the background. Not unusual, but... strange. In the lulls in conversation, I almost thought I heard the faint sound of a waterfall.

"No," she answered. "Everywhere's within walking distance, and we rarely see the need to venture into normal territory. Also, the technology issues."

"You have adapted computers, though, right? And TV?"

"Sure. The internet is essential these days. But transportation isn't necessary when we have our own methods of getting around."

I arched a brow. "Tell me it doesn't involve flying."

"Okay, I won't tell you."

"Can *I* fly? Don't fairies have wings?" Would I ever feel normal amongst these not-normals?

"You know, some do." She looked thoughtful. "Definitely something to look into. But we don't fly on broomsticks most of the time—generally we use transportation spells instead. They take more preparation, but are better designed for the weather. Too many stories of witches being blown off course into the mountains, or the sea."

I bit the inside of my cheek to avoid laughing at the mental image of a witch on a stick of wood being hurled over the Atlantic Ocean. "Makes sense. Modern world meets magic. I like it."

This place had grown on me already. I might have wound up way out of my depth, but I felt more certainty, more *alive*, than I ever had before in my life. It had been easier thinking of myself as the awkward foster kid who didn't fit in anywhere, but I hadn't come here just to keep on living the same life as I had before. Difficult or not, this new life was a chance at a real fresh start. I could be someone else entirely —witch or fairy, it didn't matter.

6

My resolution didn't last. Firstly, I woke with a jolt when a cat paw swatted at my head. I'd been forewarned about Roald's personal space issues, but still yelped when he dug his claws in after I rolled over and tried to go back to sleep. At least I'd been blessed with no hangover despite the oddly named cocktails I'd consumed at the pub last night.

Alissa sat at the kitchen table, sipping from a mug with a picture of a kitten on it. Her real-life cat padded over to her, and she stroked his head. "He didn't wake you, did he?"

"Yep." I tugged my sleeve down over my clawed-up arm. "I slept better than I expected."

"That's probably because of the cocktails. They contain special additions to help you sleep."

"Wow. That's real magic."

Showing up for work hungover would not help my case if the boss found out I wasn't a witch, so I was glad to have been spared. I felt like I'd met half the town by now, which only made me more reluctant to leave. I'd never met so many people wanting to buy me drinks, so there was little chance of ending up six feet under a tower of debt before I'd even been paid. But not if my good luck streak took a nosedive into the lake when I told the boss the truth.

"Try one of these." She tossed me a breakfast bar in a bright green wrapper. "It's an energy booster with a hint of motivation."

"Thanks. Any chance of something that will bring me luck to stop the boss from showing me the door when she finds out I'm a fairy?" I asked, taking a bite. The delicious combination of apple and cinnamon exploded in my mouth. "I get the impression I was hired to fill a spot vacated by a witch, only I'm not one."

"You won't get fired for that," said Alissa. "Also, I don't know if Bethan warned you about those lucky lattes from the local cafe, but they wear off alarmingly fast and don't tend to pay much attention to other people's luck. Besides," she added. "You belong here."

Maybe if I kept repeating the same line in my head, I'd come to believe it.

"Why am I the only fairy?" I asked. "I didn't meet any last night, and half the town was there."

"You're not," she said. "There are brownies working for the rich families... trolls... not that you're anything like them."

"I should bloody hope not," I said.

They probably don't normally abandon their children, either. Stories I'd read about fairies involved them stealing other people's children instead, but I decided not to bring that up. I had the distinct impression that the stories I'd grown up with had skipped over the realities of the paranormal world.

"Wait—Fairy Falls." I put down the breakfast bar. "Is this town—were there fairies living here before?"

"That's just a name," she said. "Madame Grey and some of the others know the founding story better than I do. It's your

57

magic we want to pin down. You mentioned you can tell what type of paranormal someone is without even looking at them. I don't know if that's a fairy talent, but maybe that's a good place to start."

I'd told her about my unexpected talent over drinks last night. "Yeah. It's like I get an image of them in my head. But that's the only power I've shown signs of. I guess I won't get to start learning magic after all, if nobody knows how fairies' magic works."

She picked up her coffee mug. "You can still learn magical theory, if you're interested. It can't hurt to know a few things if you're going to be staying here. Anyway, you definitely have some latent power, if it awakened that quickly. You can sense the truth of a person. They say the first fairies weren't able to lie at all."

"I can lie." I made a career—or a hundred attempts at a career—out of it, actually. But that was then. Here, I didn't feel the need to pretend. If nothing else, that was refreshing.

———

Once I got to work, it was to find a huge list of new names to call on my desk.

"Where's the boss?" I asked Bethan, who had an equally high stack of papers.

"In a meeting," she said around the pen between her teeth. "Check the bottom file."

I lifted the papers and found three files. "Is this…?"

"I got the information you asked for," she said in a low voice. "The files on the three candidates who were interviewed by Mr Bayer."

"Thank you." I'd invited two of them over for interviews, which had seemed a spectacular idea yesterday. Now, though, I had to wonder if that mood-altering coffee hadn't removed some vital part of my mental functions. Like the ability to judge whether it was a good idea to invite potential murderers into the office, for instance. "I should think about what to ask them. I can't exactly start with *did you murder Mr Bayer?* He died by poisoning, so I suppose anyone could have done it, right?"

"In theory," she said. "But the poison was in the coffee mug he left in his office, which was locked at the time. The same room he interviewed the potential employees in, according to the reports. Because he wasn't found dead until the next morning, they don't know how much time elapsed between the interviews and his death."

"He was alone in there? Nobody thought to check?"

"He wasn't married, didn't have children, and was by all accounts obsessed with work. It's very sad." She balanced the files in her hand while she peered at my computer screen. "I did warn Callie to keep an eye out. Who's the first candidate?"

I checked the name on the email. "He's apparently called Wilfred Bloom. Is that his real name?"

"Yes. His parents really are that posh. A total spoilt brat from what I've heard. Might have felt entitled to the position for that reason."

"Enough to murder someone?"

"He's not a strong lead, according to the police," said Bethan. "Mostly because he's a magical dud, according to his records. Born into a prestigious magical family with only bare traces of any gift, and dropped out of university after one term."

"And might he be bitter or angry?" I asked.

"Maybe. You seem to be good at reading people. He also definitely went shopping at Mr Bayer's place, the week before he applied to the position."

I raised an eyebrow. "Sounds a bit early to prepare to murder someone if you didn't get the job."

"How do you think killers' minds work?"

"No idea, thankfully. I'll have to speak to him first. Are the police okay with this?"

"He's not on the suspect list any longer," she said. "Not dangerous... I don't think. But I'd be careful."

"So he's coming in an hour."

"I'll keep an eye on the clock. Oh, I heard about last night, by the way, and it's cool that you're a fairy. I won't hold it against you. Any magic type is good for the atmosphere. I actually think a fairy might be even *more* lucky."

Hmm. I somehow doubted Blythe would agree. At least she seemed to be ignoring me today. But if she could read my thoughts... ack. *Don't think about that.*

Aloud, I said, "I should get these phone calls done before the wizard shows up."

———

I finished up my last call and put the file aside, preparing to go and meet this so-called wizard. En route, I picked up some coffee. I had a feeling I was going to need it. Not that the phone calls were particularly strenuous, but every time someone answered, my weird sixth sense insisted on bombarding me with images of their paranormal species. Werewolves, vampires, even a troll or two. A potential murderer, though? I needed all the fortifying energy I could get.

Worse than a potential murderer, if possible, was Blythe, who stood next to my desk wearing a winning smile as though she'd picked up on my train of thought. Which she probably had. "Hey, fairy."

"You know that's not actually an insult to me, don't you?" I said. "What *is* your problem?"

"You're killing our vibe." Her eyes glittered with malice. "You're not even a witch. You're a pretender."

"I'm not a pretender if I'm perfectly aware of what I am." Even though I wasn't. But the point still stood. "Excuse me. I have to interview a client."

Thankfully, she stood aside to let me pass. Callie's voice drifted in from the lobby. *There he is.* My heart drummed with nerves. Interviewing a potential murderer, even one with a ridiculous name, had seemed fine in theory... not so much in practice.

I expected a wizard to look a cross between Gandalf and Harry Potter. This guy looked more like the unholy outcome of a union between a broom and a leather couch. Unnecessary levels of leather, and his hair looked like he'd never combed it in his life. He smelled oily, and if I'd run into him in another context, I'd have slowly backed away. Not least because his eyes were such a vivid shade of purple, he must be wearing contact lenses.

"Welcome to Eldritch & Co's office. You must be Wilfred." I showed him into the interview room.

"Nice place." He planted himself in *my* interviewing chair. It'd been mine for all of five minutes, but still.

"Thank you. Can you please move to the other chair?"

I needed to let him know I was in charge. *Relax. You're a witch. A fairy. Whichever.*

"Right." He slumped into the other seat, leaving mine smelling of oil. Ugh. "What's this about?"

I perched on the edge of the seat. "You know you're here for a job interview, don't you?"

"Yeah."

I couldn't imagine why he'd got rejected from the last

one. "So, you're interested in spellcrafting positions. Can you tell me why?"

"Dunno."

"You'll need to give me some details if I'm to get your application ready. Your records…"

Actually, his records made *me* look like a stable employee. He hadn't lasted in a job longer than two weeks, and his CV had more holes than a piece of cheese. The paper smelled about as bad. Most employers would toss it away immediately.

"Yeah?" he said.

I resisted the urge to thwack him on the head with the file in order to get a non-monosyllabic answer out of him. "I'm here to get you a job, and to be frank, it sounds like you don't want one."

"I need one. Just not the ones you keep emailing me about. I don't do spellcrafting."

Apparently, he didn't mind people knowing he wasn't magically accomplished. "We have it on record that you used our services several times, including last week when you were interviewed by Mr Bayer."

His brow wrinkled. "Bayer? He died, right?"

"Yes. A few days ago. Did you want to work for him? Because if you aren't interested in any of the positions we're offering, you can request others, or…" *Stop wasting my time.* "Find something more suitable."

He scuffed the floor with the toe of his boot, which was polished black with some fancy-looking dials on the side. "Do you have any idea who my mother is?"

I'd skimmed his file long enough to work out his place in the scheme of things. "It sounds like she's a powerful witch. But you didn't inherit the gift?"

"No."

A prickling sensation travelled across my shoulder blades. *He lied.*

I knew it as surely as I'd known the last client was a werewolf from the phone call. What was I now, a lie detector? I looked down at the file in my hand. He was listed as a magical dud, but he kept being pressured into applying for jobs which required a high magic skill level. None indicated he *didn't* have powerful magic. And his mother sure seemed interested in pushing him into making the best use of his talents.

"Are you sure?"

"If you knew my mother, you'd know she wants me to work in the spellcrafting business and nothing else," he said. "I'm doing this to get her off my back."

"So you don't actually want to be a spellcrafter?" I had limited sympathy for people who had been given every advantage possible in life yet acted like total brats, but on the other hand, maybe I saw why he kept resisting. His mother should have cut off his allowance. Now that'd be more of an incentive.

"No," he said.

"Then let me help you find something more suitable." I lifted the file on the pretext of rereading it, while debating how to get back to the topic of Mr Bayer's untimely death. "What do you enjoy doing? You must have ambitions."

I expected another monosyllabic response. Instead, he said, "I don't want to be an official wizard. I want… I kind of want to open my own bakery." He looked down as though embarrassed.

"I can help with that," I said. "But you need to brush up on your interview technique. Also, you might want to wash off the smell on your CV. It's a little off-putting."

He smirked. "It's a spell designed to repel people."

You probably don't need it, to be honest. "Overkill," I said to him. "Believe me. Just being honest is enough."

"You think I haven't *told* my mother? She doesn't care."

Truth. It wasn't just that his words rang with sincerity—I *knew* he spoke the truth. The same way I'd known the next interviewee was a werewolf. But did my apparent ability to detect whether people were magical or not extend to being able to tell if they were innocent of a crime?

"We normally encourage clients to play to their strengths," I said. But competence did not equal interest. I could play the piano, but had zero interest in taking up lessons. "I think we both know you're underplaying your real talents, and that's not helping. What's your magical gift?"

"Memory. I can read a book and then recite it back to you word for word. I've never had to study for a test in my life."

My brewing sympathy evaporated. "You poor thing." Oops. Professional face on, Blair.

"I'm a grade five wizard," he muttered. "Yes, I know that's the top level, and no, I'm not interested in using those talents at all. Having a good memory has no practical use whatsoever. I don't want to spend the rest of my life in stuffy classrooms or magical workshops."

"Did you tell that to Mr Bayer?" I asked.

"I'm pretty sure he knew soon as he saw me. What does it matter?"

"It matters because he was murdered," I said.

His face went purple. "You think I—I've been a pacifist since I was a kid. The whole reason I didn't want to work with him is because you have to use live toads and rabbits in some of his spells and I wouldn't do it." He gave me a defiant stare.

He's telling the truth.

Okay. This was too far. I couldn't read minds, let alone tell if people were lying. I thought witches had only *one* primary talent—but nobody had said anything about fairies having the same limitation.

"All right," I said. "You also look a little intimidating in all that leather. That, combined with your lack of cooperation… can you blame me for getting a little on edge? I'm new here."

"Fine." He folded his arms. "So the police have no leads on the killer?"

"No. Only that he was poisoned at some point on the day of the interview… hence the questions. When your name came up on our call list for this week, I felt I had to check."

"Oh." His expression cleared. "I don't know anything. I left immediately after the interview."

"When you were at the interview, did you see anything strange?" I asked. "I have a couple of the other clients coming in for interviews today and I'd like to be forewarned if they're dangerous."

He bowed his head. "I didn't see anything, but you might want to talk to Vaughn, the other candidate. He threw a real temper tantrum after he got rejected. Cursed up a storm."

"What, you mean actually conjured up a storm?" I asked warily. He was the guy who my weird sixth sense had identified as a werewolf, so probably not.

"No. Yelled a lot. Got kicked out by Mr Bayer's security."

But didn't turn into a wolf? "Call the office again if you remember anything else, okay?"

As I showed him out, Bethan signalled to me to come over to her. After closing the door, I walked to her desk.

"I overheard part of the interview," she said. "Looked him up. Looks like his mother does want him to go into the spell-craft business, but nothing about what *he* wants. But he certainly seems to have a thing against animal cruelty. He's given most of his wealth to charitable causes."

So he had told the truth. But could I trust my instincts? "Do fairies have the ability to tell if people are lying or not?"

"Wait—did that happen to you?"

"I'm not sure. But I knew he wasn't lying when he said he didn't want the job. He also said the werewolf dude was angry about not getting it and threw some kind of tantrum."

"Wait—he's the one coming over this afternoon?"

I nodded. "I handled a wizard, so a werewolf shouldn't be a problem."

At least, I hoped not.

7

I t was considerably more difficult to focus on my job after the interview. Partly because of my upcoming second interview that afternoon, and also because during every phone call, I still kept getting images and impressions of everyone's paranormal type, along with uncomfortable prickling sensations whenever they said something that was less than truthful.

I'd come to learn very quickly that people lied. A lot. They ranged from little white lies to full-on fabrications. I was sympathetic to these people, because being paranormal doubtless meant fewer opportunities if they were a smaller population and they all got on in the normal world as badly as I had. It wasn't like I hadn't bluffed my way through a few dozen interviews myself, but when I'd worked in recruitment with regular people, I hadn't had the nagging sixth sense blaring in my ear every time someone told a fib. Knowingly sending unqualified people into dangerous positions didn't seem a wise thing to do either, but it really did make doing my job difficult.

During my afternoon break before the interview, I went

downstairs to forewarn Callie. I figured one of the others had updated her by now, but I'd check in case I was violating any rules without being aware of it.

"Hi," said Callie, looking up from the reception desk as I walked past. "I heard you're having an eventful day. Was that wizard who walked in a client?"

"Yeah," I said. "Speaking of clients—did Bethan tell you we're interviewing a werewolf yet?"

"She mentioned it, but she said he's not with the pack." She moved a stack of papers across the desk. "I'll be able to sense what he is if we meet face to face."

"Really?" I asked.

"We can always tell. You haven't met the pack yet?"

"No." I'd mostly met witches and wizards last night. "There's just one pack?"

"One pack of werewolves. We're like family."

So this guy had defied the trend if he hadn't disclosed what he was. "Did Bethan also mention that he might be slightly unstable?"

"That he's a murder suspect? I can hear you through the office door, you know." She looked more amused than annoyed. "I won't envy you if Veronica finds out. How unstable, exactly?"

"I don't know," I admitted. "He seemed fine on the phone, but supposedly got into a heated argument with one of the other interviewees at Mr Bayer's place. So I want to be prepared. How would I go about protecting myself against an angry werewolf?"

"Silver," she said. "Anything made out of pure silver. You might want to ask security. He helped us update our defences after the murder."

"Nathan's still here?" When he'd said he used to apprehend misbehaving paranormals, he'd included fairies on that list. I hoped I didn't qualify as misbehaving.

"I called him in to look out for trouble, considering the interesting clientele you're interviewing today."

Touché. "So… if he *does* shift, I throw silver in his face?"

"Yes, but if you carry it on you all the time, he might feel threatened," she said. "We have highly developed senses, especially smell. He'll be able to tell if you have silver, so don't make it look like an outright threat. Luckily, the office is full of innocent-looking items that fit the bill."

"Maybe I'll hit him with the stapler if he attacks me. Or can I have some handcuffs?"

"None here. Security… I wouldn't ask for those. I down-played the fact that our visitor is a murder suspect, but I think he knows."

"He's not the police, though, right? I'm kind of lost on what a paranormal hunter actually does."

Her friendly smile disappeared. "He's not one. But they're more of an independent collective for policing paranormals who live outside of the boundaries. That wolf *might* qualify, but since there aren't any active hunters in town, he'll be handed over to the police."

Ah. There was probably some history between the were-wolves and the hunters that I didn't know about yet.

"Sorry, I was just curious."

"Not to worry." She smiled again. "If he's not a rogue, he won't have anything to worry about. Rogues are rare because they tend to have good reason to get kicked out of a pack."

Uneasiness flickered through me. It didn't sound like this guy had told anyone he was a werewolf to begin with, but if he *was* a rogue, who even knew what he was capable of?

"But if he's a rogue," she added, "it makes no sense for him to be applying for jobs at wizard shops. None at all. It's not a very good cover story if you look closely enough."

"Nobody would know he's a werewolf at all if I hadn't accidentally seen through him, right?" I said. "Or is it due to pure luck and cleverness that he's managed to stay hidden?"

"If he met one of us in person, we'd be able to sniff him out," she said. "I'd guess he's lying low amongst other paranormals who wouldn't guess what he is. None of us would apply to work in spellcraft. We can't use magic like the witches or wizards can."

"If he wants to avoid attention, getting involved in a murder case in any way is bound to put the spotlight on him."

Or maybe he was covering up. Poison wasn't an obvious murder weapon choice for someone who could transform into a hairy monster. Whether or not he actively wanted anyone to know that.

"Speak of the devil," said Callie.

I jumped, thinking she meant the wolf. Instead, the front door opened and Nathan walked in.

"I heard you were running interviews," he said. "Something about a stray werewolf."

Well, hello to you, too. "Yes, we are."

"A rogue werewolf? I suppose you wouldn't know the difference yet, but rogues—"

"Are werewolves without a pack. Callie told me."

"And a murder suspect?"

Ah. Callie had been dead right—there was no way he wouldn't guess. "Not according to the police."

Nathan tilted his head. "Have you spoken to the police?"

"Nope," I said. "Don't worry, you won't have to arrest anyone." Or maybe he would. Despite his brusqueness, I wouldn't mind having him outside the door when the werewolf came in.

"Including the man you interviewed this morning?"

Note to self: don't bother trying to fool a paranormal hunter. "Not a suspect," I said, in my best *client info is confi-*

dential tone. "I thought you arrested misbehaving paranormals, not slightly deceptive wizards with dreadful fashion sense. He was about as dangerous as a toothless badger."

His brows rose in puzzlement. "Werebadgers are a nasty territorial bunch. I wouldn't necessarily say losing their teeth would make much of a difference."

"It was the first thing that came into my head," I said, wishing I could staple my lips closed. "You're not going to scare off the clients, are you?"

There was a muffled laugh. Callie's head was hidden behind her computer screen, but I gave her a look. "You know the boss wouldn't want us scaring people away."

She sighed. "Let him in. Nathan, stand outside and look intimidating. He wouldn't guess *I'm* the one who can sniff him out, unless he knows I'm the pack leader's daughter."

"I wouldn't be surprised if he did," Nathan said. "If you're going to keep inviting murder suspects in, sooner or later the police will end up involved. Fair warning."

"We have all their names and details," I said. "Plus the whole office is made up of witches, and we can drag up any info on them in a second. Can the police do that?" Clients who sneakily hid their own identities in plain sight might require a more subtle approach.

Okay, and I also hated abandoning a problem. I would help the wizard find a more suitable position. Not just because it was my job, but because I hated not having closure. It gave me something to focus on besides my own magic, or lack thereof, and the absence of answers on my magical history.

"This isn't the world you knew, Blair," he said. "Not to imply you don't belong here, but there are rules you simply won't have had the chance to learn yet."

"Exactly," I said. "He'll never suspect I know what he is." Even I didn't quite know why my powers had chosen now to manifest, nor why I could suddenly sense lies. I doubted even the police could do that.

"Be careful," said Nathan. "Playing games with the pack never ends well."

I supposed he'd know. What had led him to retire from monster hunting and take up a position of security in a quiet town like this? It wasn't any of my business, but I did wonder. The slightly irritable expression on Callie's face suggested now was not the time to pursue that line of questioning.

"I'll keep that in mind, but it'd look suspicious if we cancel now." I spotted a male figure approaching across the cobbled street. "There he is. Nobody act suspicious." I glanced at Nathan, who was scowling. "As far as he's concerned, he's on the way to a job interview, not an interrogation. Besides, if we scare him off, the police might lose a potential suspect."

"I'll be waiting outside," Nathan said pointedly, and I backed into the office, trying to compose myself.

The place still smelled of the wizard's spell, while there was a sudden abundance of silver objects on every work surface. Bethan gave me an innocent smile from behind a pile of staples. I grabbed a handful and shoved them into my pocket, as I heard Callie's greeting from the reception area. Drawing in a breath, I went back out to greet the new interviewee.

A young man with shaggy dark hair walked in. I wouldn't have guessed him for a werewolf immediately, but there was something undeniably animal-like about the way he moved.

I hitched on a smile, which immediately slid off when he entered our office. "This place stinks of oil."

Ah. He could smell the last interviewee. In fairness, you didn't have to be a werewolf to pick up on the stench of whatever spell he'd been using.

"This way," I said, beckoning him into the side office. Apparently Vaughn Llewellyn was going to be even less polite than the last guy, which didn't bother me too much. I'd spent long enough being screamed at in customer service positions to develop an effective poker face and the ability to defuse situations. Or if all else failed, duck for cover. On the other hand, the fact that he was a werewolf threw a new sense of danger into the mix.

I casually felt for the staples in my pocket, hoping I wouldn't need them, closed the door behind him and took a seat. "Hello, Mr Llewellyn."

He grunted. As professional as the last guy, then. "Where's the boss?"

"Busy. So I'm doing the interview instead." I plastered on a smile faker than the wizard's contact lenses. "If you don't mind, I'd like to ask you some questions about your qualifications."

Vaughn scowled, leaning back in the seat. "I'm qualified."

Really. If he'd told a lie as big as not being a werewolf, I doubted the other information in his file were accurate, either.

"You're a grade four spellcaster," I went on. "Can you tell me the most common types of grade four spell?" I'd asked for Bethan's help devising some convincing questions in order to find out the extent of his lies without being too obvious.

A muscle ticked in his jaw. "Why is that relevant?"

"You're applying for a spellcasting position." Maybe poking the beast wasn't such a great idea after all. "Our policy is to match people up with what they're suited best for. You have no previous experience, so we'll have to go with what you know."

"All right," he muttered. "I don't know. Happy?"

"Haven't you trained as a wizard? Your CV says you

studied at the Lancashire University of Spellcraft. So if I searched the university's list of alumni, I'd find your name?"

His scowl deepened. I didn't even need to pretend to grow more suspicious with every word he said—or didn't say.

"Nothing wrong with embellishing the truth," he said.

"There's embellishing the truth, and there's outright lying," I said, tensing when his eyes narrowed.

"You called me here to make fun of me, didn't you? Fine. I don't have magic. Happy?"

"Then why did you apply to spellcasting positions? You must know you'd lose out to a certified wizard."

"Certified wizard?" His eyes narrowed. "Wait. That idiot wizard was in here, wasn't he? The place smells of him."

Oh no. I should have moved to a different office.

I released a breath. Slowly. "We had Mr Bloom in here for an interview earlier. We often invite our potential candidates here to work on their applications and skills."

"He doesn't want to work as a spellcrafter either. Wants to open a bakery or some nonsense like that." He still wore an irritated scowl, but didn't look on the verge of shifting into a wolf and ripping my throat out.

"Did he tell you that?" I asked.

"He wouldn't stop mouthing off while we were in the interview room."

Hmm. "He mentioned you," I said. "Said you two got into a fight."

He gave me an incredulous look. "You invited me here to talk about that pathetic excuse for a wizard?"

"Both your names were on my list before I realised the connection," I said—technically true. But if he wasn't qualified as a spellcaster, he could no more have committed a magical murder than transformed into a spoon. "But now you mention it—why pick a fight with him?"

"He's an idiot. The boss died, right? That's why you're questioning me." He rose to his feet. "I'm not here to be insulted. I dunno *why* I'm here, to be honest."

I sat up straight, my heart rate kicking up. "If you were innocent, you wouldn't be making a break for it. We have a lot of silver in the office and a trained paranormal hunter on security duty."

Vaughn fell back into the seat. "This isn't necessary. I didn't kill anyone. As you know by now, I'm not magical at all. I might as well have…"

Turned into a wolf and attacked him? "Anyone can use poison. If they know what they're doing."

"Not that type," he said. "Didn't you read the newspaper? It said the poisonous leaves came from his own garden. The whole place is covered in security spells. I didn't smell any poison in the interview room while I was there, so it must have happened afterwards."

Werewolf senses. More to the point, the so-called lie detector that had been blaring in my head all afternoon had gone suspiciously quiet. So was he telling the truth?

"Then why did you throw a tantrum after being rejected?" I asked.

"Because that wizard made fun of my haircut." He scowled again. "And because the guy who was going to get it was a complete tool."

"Which guy?"

"Simeon Clarke."

Hmm. "If you have any more information—"

"I don't."

"The receptionist, Callie, is willing to help you if you don't want to confide in me. I take my job very seriously, Mr Llewellyn."

There was nothing more to say. He hadn't lied, or my magical lie detector was broken. Either way, I needed more details on the actual murder before I made any more assumptions.

He took that as an invitation to leave and stormed out of the office. I heard a door slam behind him. *Another suspect down.*

"Sounds like that went well," said Bethan, entering the interview room behind me. "What's the verdict?"

I lowered his file and got to my feet. "Apparently the poison was applied after he left, because he'd have sniffed it out otherwise. Also, he claims that it came from Mr Bayer's own garden. I must have missed that part of the article."

"Might be lying," said Bethan. "I was on the verge of calling security in, but it looks like his bark is worse than his bite."

"That depends if he comes storming back here to start a fight with me when he realises why I sent him to speak to Callie if he wants to confide in someone."

"Ah." She nodded. "Good idea... possibly. Callie can handle herself, but if the pack gets involved... things could get nasty."

I groaned. "I'm sorry. It sort of slipped out. I didn't give away any other hints that I know what he is."

"Good. Did *he* give away anything at all?"

"Well, he said I should question this Simeon Clarke next. Apparently he's the person who'd have got the job if Mr Bayer hadn't died."

"Hmm." She paused. "I suppose it's worth calling him. I think the police dismissed him as a suspect."

"Like the wizard," I said. "Who else have the police questioned—?"

There was an almighty crash. My heart jumped into my throat. "Oh god. He turned into a wolf, didn't he?"

Bethan ran from the office with me on her heels, skidding

to a halt in the reception area. Vaughn had gone, while Callie was dusting her hands off, a scowl on her pretty face.

"What happened?" I asked.

"He didn't take my generous offer of help very well." Her voice deepened while her face briefly disappeared beneath a coating of thick grey fur. Her jaw lengthened, curved teeth sprouting from her gums, and I wanted to slowly back away. There was a total disconnect between the smiley receptionist and this terrifying monster.

"Sorry," said Bethan, to Callie. "Did he hurt you?"

"No," she said, in a growly voice. "I punched the desk. And now I can't turn back. I always have trouble the week after the full moon… I'm scaring you, aren't I, Blair?"

Yes. "No. I'm glad that guy didn't shift and attack us."

"No, he just used some very colourful language."

"What *is* going on here?" Veronica strode out of her office into the reception area, her gaze sweeping across all of us and landing on Callie's furred face. Lucky the rest of her hadn't transformed, too.

"Disagreement with a client," said Callie, her teeth slipping into wolf form and back to human again. "Sorry."

"*Which* client?" Her gaze was on me. *Ah. I still haven't told her I'm not a witch.* Now did not seem like a spectacular time to bring that up.

"Vaughn Llewellyn," I said. "It was my idea to invite him for an interview. Apparently my magical talent allows me to sense whether people are paranormal or not, so when I spoke to him on the phone and got an impression of a were-wolf and not a wizard, I wanted to see if I was right. He was on the call list anyway."

I held my breath as her eyes narrowed. *Please, please don't fire me.* If I had to leave, I might never know who my family had been. I'd be exiled to the human world, doomed to bounce between jobs leaving chaos behind me. I *liked* Fairy

Falls. I liked the others—except Blythe—and even answering calls was a thousand times better than the night shift or fifteen-hour call centre shifts or… anything.

She looked accusingly at Bethan. "Werewolves in the office again? It's always you, isn't it?"

Not the reaction I'd expected. "Wait," I said. "I said it was my idea…"

"This scheme has my daughter written all over it," said Veronica. "Let me guess—she used a divining spell."

"Has this happened before?" I asked, confused.

"Not exactly," Bethan admitted, her face reddening. "But there have been… incidents. We're paranormals, so are our clients. Occasionally they start fights in the office or…"

"Set things on fire," said the boss. "Once she decided it was her duty to find a position for the town's resident pyromaniac. She likes taking on hopeless cases."

No wonder she'd fought so hard to get *me* to stay. "So I'm not being fired?"

"If you were, I'd have to fire the whole office," said Veronica. "Where Bethan goes, so does Lizzie. And Blythe can read minds, so she has no excuse for not warning me."

Blythe glowered at me. Someone still thought it was my fault, then.

Veronica looked at Callie and sighed. "Where is security?"

"Following the werewolf," said Callie, in a low growly voice.

The boss checked her watch. "Given the circumstances, it's probably best if you all leave early."

8

Anyone might have gone home for a nap after the day I'd had, but thanks to the wolf incident, adrenaline zipped through my nerve-endings, in dire need of an outlet. And today's interviews had sparked more questions than ever. It was late afternoon, but not too late for me to take a walk over to Mr Bayer's shop and have a poke around.

I'd read the newspaper article and learnt that he was a widower with no children and few close friends, none with a motive for murder. Most had already been questioned. I shouldn't even be going there, but while my abilities might only extend to being able to sniff out lies and magical disguises, but I couldn't help wondering if someone else had sneaked into the interview room and planted the poison there. Since the hospital where Alissa worked was down the high street from Mr Bayer's place, I figured I could at least have a look until she finished work.

The high street was right out of a picture book. Buildings of stone rather than brick, with old-fashioned signs. They didn't seem to have any of the normal world's high street brands or chain stores. I still needed to do some proper grocery shopping, but most places had 'we only take cash' signs in the windows. I barely had enough spare cash for bus fare. There were ATMs and even a bank, but when I put my card into the cash machine's slot, it came up with an error message. Then smoke poured out of the slot. *Oh no.* I yanked the card free. The back of it had entirely melted.

"That won't work here," said a passing witch.

"But—all my money is in my account." All twenty-five pence of it. "How am I getting paid?"

The witch blinked owlish eyes at me. "Everyone is set up with a local bank account here. You're the new girl, right?"

"Yep." I vaguely remembered Alissa mentioning something like that between cocktails last night, but the details were fuzzy. I stuck my ruined credit card back into my bag and carried on walking down the cobbled street. Every time I thought I'd started to get the hang of my new life, a new problem reared its head. In fairness, the same could be said for life in general—*there it is.* I stopped beside the sign that said *Mr Bayer, Spellmaker.* Spellmakers apparently made handmade "spells" for the general public, their purposes ranging from practical jokes to useful things like pens with endless ink or hair-straightening combs. I walked past the shop as casually as I dared. Doors closed, windows shuttered. The interview had apparently taken place in the office upstairs, since the candidates had been tested on magical abilities and Mr Bayer hadn't wanted to accidentally break any windows. I squinted up at the first floor, tilting my head. Pity my ability to sense magical abilities didn't extend to being able to see through solid objects—

The door slammed open and a huge figure shouldered his way out. Not werewolf-huge, but human-shaped. Like a big human. A really big human with wings. Images of stone cliff faces paraded through my head as I took a careful step backwards, but he'd already spotted me.

"Who are you?" he demanded.

"I'm Blair," I said. "Who are you? Wasn't someone murdered in that shop? What are you doing in there?"

"I'm the chief of police, and it's a crime scene. So *you're* the one questioning all my suspects."

Oops. "I didn't know you were with the police. You're not wearing a badge or uniform."

He scowled. "I'm undercover."

I suppressed a laugh, more out of relief that he wasn't the killer than anything else. Undercover? He barely fit through the doors.

"Something amusing?" he asked, cracking his stone-like knuckles.

I shook my head. "No. Absolutely not." For a second, the image in my mind's eye flickered, showing something huge, winged and grey. His real form? "Are you a shapeshifter? Or…" What else had wings? "A fairy?"

His teeth bared. "*Gargoyle.*"

Of course—Alissa had said. "Easy mistake to make." I attempted a smile. "I'm new here."

"I'm aware of that," he said. "It's lucky Madame Grey's granddaughter seems to have adopted you. You have a lot to learn about the paranormal laws. We're not known for letting criminals off lightly. The laws are hard."

Hard as stone. No kidding.

"I got curious," I said. "Like I said—I'm new in town. I've never been to a spellcraft shop before."

"And you just happened to walk past this particular store?"

"Because it's the only one I've heard of."

"Do you make a habit of going to murder sites in the normal world?"

"Nope. Definitely not."

So that's why the others hadn't called the police to the office. Even a werewolf would be utterly dwarfed by this brute, even in human form. His attitude did not help in the slightest.

He took a step closer so that he loomed over me. "Stay out of this case, Miss Wilkes. This is paranormal business, not yours."

"Hey, Blair." Alissa waved at me from across the street. I gladly turned my back and walked over to her, ignoring the gargoyle's stony—ha—glare behind me.

"What a lovely guy," I said to Alissa.

"Isn't he? Roald peed on his feet once."

I burst out laughing. "I would literally pay money to witness that. Or I would, if my credit card hadn't melted."

"Ah. I should have warned you not to use it here. Why was he angry with you, anyway?"

"I'm new here and I accidentally stole his case," I said. "Can the police tell if people are lying? By magical means?"

"No," she said. "What do you mean, stole his case?"

"Accidentally questioned two of his suspects. Well. It started as an accident. It's been an interesting day. And I know I shouldn't have wandered over to Mr Bayer's shop, but I didn't know he was in there."

She eyed him over my shoulder. "You're going to make his life difficult, I can tell."

"You say that like it's a good thing."

"Nobody likes Steve. Unfortunately, he's the best at catching and intimidating criminals."

"He seems to have missed this one. I thought he was the killer when he came out of the shop."

"That probably didn't help," she said. "By the way, I spoke to Madame Grey. She's ruled that you *are* magical, and that you're to be tested for other abilities so we can pin down your likely talent."

"Tested?" I said warily. "In what way?"

"In whatever way she decides."

Oh boy.

———

I stood outside in the rain, hands spread to the sky. Rainwater drenched me, and no matter how clearly I pictured the clouds parting, they stubbornly refused to.

"I don't think this is going to work," I said through chattering teeth.

"Focus." Bangles rattled as Rita pointed imperiously to the sky.

I tried to focus, but the only thing I could think about was getting indoors as fast as possible. I didn't think standing outside in a storm was going to jump-start my powers. Even here, the rain turned the roads into mud-drenched hazards. The rain was the first normal thing I'd seen since I'd arrived.

Supposedly weather-working was common to both witches and some fairies, and since my other ability had awakened without warning, Madame Grey thought I needed an extra incentive. She claimed not to be treating me differently to the other witches, but nobody else was standing outside in the cold, and I doubted people like Blythe were subjected to this indignity. Rita had volunteered herself as my new tutor, and took the job seriously. Very seriously.

I shivered again, water tracing its way down the back of my shirt. "I'm focusing. It's not happening."

"I suppose not." She sounded disappointed. "Come back inside."

She beckoned me back into the witches' place, which

happened to be the site of the evening classes for the witches who took them. Thankfully there weren't a dozen curious witches in the empty classroom she'd picked out, and when she pointed her wand at me, the water entirely disappeared from my clothes. Now I saw that she'd somehow remained dry throughout the entire ordeal. I made a mental note to ask how to cast that spell, then remembered I might not get a wand at all.

"It's possible that you have an elemental power," said Rita. She snapped her fingers, with the clank of bangles. "Look at this pen."

I looked at the pen which she'd conjured to her hand. It didn't transform or float or start talking or anything, though none of those things would have surprised me by now. But the pen looked like an ordinary ballpoint.

"Imagine it bursting into flames."

I watched the pen. "If I could make things burst into flames, it'd probably have been triggered during my last customer service job."

"Vindictiveness isn't becoming of a witch."

"I'm not one," I said. Also, Blythe was a shining example of vindictiveness hidden behind a pretty face. "Isn't my truth-sensing ability enough on its own?" I was actually keen to learn more—though perhaps not in such a hands-on way.

"None of us has enough experience to tutor you in that," she said. "Besides, it's a reactive ability. It runs on autopilot for you, by the sounds of things."

"Only since I came here," I said. "Maybe I'm a defective paranormal from living with humans for so long."

"There's no such thing." She flicked her wand and the pen vanished. "Your normal upbringing will shift in time. You've had your whole world uprooted."

"You don't have to try so hard for me." Unorthodox lessons aside, the witches had made me feel welcome despite not being one of them. "Anyway, this is possibly the best thing that ever happened to me. But… I wondered. In the other paranormal towns, might there be other fairies? I mean, the same type of fairy as I am?"

Relations? Surely not. Maybe it was for the best that I didn't know. After all, whoever my real family were, they'd given me up for adoption.

Her expression softened. "Madame Grey says you're heavily glamoured. Until it's removed, we won't know your fairy type."

"I'm heavily what?" I said blankly.

"Glamoured. It means someone put a spell on you to hide your own true nature."

My stomach twisted. "You mean I could be green and hairy underneath this disguise? My boss—I haven't even told my boss I'm a fairy. It never came up."

"Your magical class and paranormal type has no bearing on your ability to do your job. It sounds like it's come in handy, if rumour is to be believed."

Rumour? *Oh no.* This had Blythe's handiwork written all over it. But it wasn't like I'd set out to deceive everyone. Besides, while my truth-sensing ability had given me a headache all day, I *had* managed to find several employees for highly specialist positions which I couldn't imagine having done without that reassuring sixth sense in my head telling me which people were trustworthy and qualified, and which were hiding secrets.

"Maybe it has," I said, "but it doesn't mean I know who my family are."

"It's not impossible to find out," she said. "What do you know of your history?"

I shook my head. "I was put up for adoption when I was a baby. I don't remember my life before, if I had one, or my parents. So unless there's a website for paranormals to connect with long-lost relatives…"

"There isn't. We're generally very close-knit, within our own villages and towns, and covens guard their secrets. I know the covens within this town, but not the others."

"Speaking of which," I said, "is there anyone here who might remember if fairies lived here twenty-five years ago?"

"Good question. Possibly some of our elder residents, but… I don't think this is where your parents lived. Someone would have recognised you."

Yeah. I guess they would. I blinked hard, angry with myself for getting my own hopes up when I'd known this conversation wouldn't end well. I couldn't even remember my first foster family. I was passed around three or four times before my third birthday, from what I'd been told, before Mr and Mrs Wilkes had taken me in. But all those families had been human. Normals.

What was so terrible about raising a child that my real family had felt the need to abandon me with normal humans? Did they really care so little? No… they must have had a reason. I'd spent my childhood making up stories about my real parents. They were superheroes hunted by a terrible villain and had to hide me to keep me safe. They were on the run from a serial killer. They had top-secret jobs and made the wrong person angry. Harmless stories took on a whole new meaning when viewed through the lens of being paranormal. It was safer to believe they'd genuinely loved me and gave me up against their will, but pursuing that train of thought would only end in tears.

I pushed the thought firmly aside and returned my attention to the magic lesson. I had a new life here in Fairy Falls, and that was enough, for now.

————

I reached work the following morning to find the others gathered in the reception area. The desk had been over-turned, papers scattered the floor, and in place of Callie was a man-sized wolf sprawled on the desk. Seeing nobody was panicking, I assumed it was Callie and not Vaughn.

"What happened?" I asked Bethan, who stood closest to her.

"Someone came in, startled her, and she shifted. And now she can't turn back."

Callie growled.

"Who came in?" I took a few steps closer to her, my heart beating faster even though I knew it was Callie. I'd had a bad experience being chased by a huge dog when I was little and since then, I'd always been wary of large furry animals.

"She can't talk in that state," said Lizzie. "She's too far gone. We have to wait for her to shift back, which might take a few hours."

"Oh." I looked at the upturned desk. "Did the intruder steal anything? Or try to get into the office?"

The wolf gave another low growl, waved a paw, and knocked over the chair. Oddly, the uncoordinated movement made her look less intimidating.

"We don't know," Bethan said. "She was the first of us to arrive here this morning. I assume she knocked the desk over, but there's no way to prove it."

Callie disentangled herself from the desk, knocking it fully upside-down in the process. She let out a growl that might have been an apology.

Bethan padded over to her, pulled out her wand, and conjured a pen and paper to her hands. "Can you draw a picture of the intruder?"

Callie's paw-like hand tried to grab the pen and nearly knocked Bethan over instead. She growled again, her fur standing on end. Even knowing what the real woman under the wolf mask looked like, I didn't want to stand too close. She was huge, and those teeth were as long as my feet, easily. I did my best to picture her as smiling and blond, not fanged and furious.

"Okay, how about I ask you some questions and you nod if I'm right?" I said. "Was the intruder male? Nod—no, growl, if I'm right."

Callie whined. *Hmm... what does that mean?*

"What is going on?" The boss walked in, her eyebrows disappearing into her hairline.

"There was an intruder," I said. "He startled Callie into shifting, and now she can't turn back."

Veronica turned to Callie. "We can't have that, can we? Shift back, Callie."

"She can't, I don't think," said Lizzie. "I'm not sure she shifted on purpose."

"What makes you say that?"

"Callie wouldn't shift unless she was being attacked," Bethan said. "Even if another werewolf came in. And if it *was* another werewolf, they'd have fought. There's no blood."

"Is anything missing?" the boss asked, eyeing the piles of papers beside the desk, drenched in spilt coffee.

"No idea." Bethan moved to start picking up the papers. "I can't imagine the intruder made it into the office with her in the way. I assume they fled when she shifted, but there's no way to tell."

The door opened and Blythe walked in. "What's going on?" Of course, her accusing stare went immediately to me.

Callie growled.

Veronica let out a long-suffering sigh. "Will you all please tidy up the mess while you wait for Callie to shift back? I assumed you were done inviting dangerous individuals into the office."

"Some of us knew better," said Blythe, continuing to glare at me as Veronica returned to her own office.

"I highly doubt it was one of the candidates who broke in," I said. "One was innocent and the other would have turned into a wolf himself if they came to blows. There aren't even any hairs on the floor. Have you reported it to the police?" I asked Bethan.

"I don't think my mother wants to," she said quietly. "She won't admit it, but the murder made her paranoid, and this won't help a bit."

No kidding. I didn't particularly want Steve the Gargoyle sniffing around and finding out just how much information I'd gathered on the murder. But the break-in added a new dimension of urgency. There were rarely fewer than three people in the building, but if one of the people we'd questioned *was* the killer, all of them knew who we were and where we worked. Maybe even where we lived.

Not a pleasant thought. At all.

"Is someone going to tell me what's going on?" Blythe demanded. "I'm taking a wild guess that *she* was involved."

"No," Bethan said. "The intruder broke in before any of us got here. Can you help us clean up?"

Callie whined and waved a paw at the discarded papers, sending them floating across the floor. I picked up several papers, but the ones soaked in coffee were a lost cause.

"She didn't have to be directly involved," Blythe said snottily. "A non-witch being here is destroying our vibe. Bad luck affects everyone in the office. It's lucky Callie was here."

Callie growled under her breath. I shot Blythe a glare and returned to the paperwork, trying to ignore her words. But the thoughts remained. Maybe the intruder *had* come here as a direct result of my meddling.

What if I really had brought bad luck down on everyone just from being a fairy and not a witch?

9

The next few hours were hectic. Firstly, we had to clean up the mess, while Bethan took Callie home to the pack until she turned human again. When she did, she'd be able to tell us who the intruder was. Then we might solve two crimes in one fell swoop. Or werewolf growl. But the atmosphere in the office was subdued all morning. Even the printer seemed gloomy, making the occasional whining noise from the corner. I didn't know how I got through two hours of phone calls, and I'd totally forgotten about my third interview until Bethan knocked on the office door, telling me there was someone to see me.

"The last suspect?" I asked. This Simeon Clarke was the guy who would have actually got the job if Mr Bayer hadn't met an untimely demise. Hardly a likely candidate for murder, but his name was on the list all the same. Apparently he was less qualified than the wizard but considerably more so than any of the other candidates. I wasn't in the mood for another interrogation, but after the break-in, I'd take any distraction I could get.

The office door opened and a smartly dressed young man walked in. *Wizard,* my sixth sense told me.

I know he's a wizard, I told the voice in my head.

He smiled. "I hope I'm not disturbing you."

"No. You're Mr Simeon Clarke, correct?" Like in his profile picture, he wore a smart suit and was polished and sophisticated-looking, in total contrast to the other two. Not suspicious at all, but my nerves were on edge. Still, we'd arranged the interview before the break-in. He'd have no reason to know… unless he was responsible.

Blythe snapped a glance onto me. "Nobody said we were inviting any more candidates in."

"That would be because you aren't the boss," I said pleasantly. "Simeon, would you come this way?"

Blythe's eyes narrowed and she rose to her feet. "I don't think this is a good idea."

"If it's not a good time, I can come back later," Simeon said. "But if you want to go back to work, we won't be long."

To my immense surprise, Blythe's angry expression entirely disappeared like a switch had been hit, and she took her seat again in an almost docile way. So manners did work on her. That, or she didn't want to smear the company's name by starting an argument with a client.

"You seem a little distracted," he commented, as we took our seats in the interview room.

"Yes, we actually had a break-in earlier."

I waited to see any signs of guilt. None came, though his smile slipped. "That's awful. I'm sorry. I can come in at a later date if that's more convenient for you?"

"No, it's fine," I said. "I misplaced my question list. I'm also new in town, so I'm still adjusting. It's my understanding that you're looking for a job in spellcraft."

"Actually, I just secured a position in magical craftwork."

"You—excuse me?"

He gave me a smile. "I actually got the job offer a few hours before I came here. But the offer was pending after my interview last Monday."

"Really? You applied for both jobs at once?"

"I applied to several positions. Mr Bayer was well-liked and paid well, it was obviously going to be a highly competitive position. I didn't expect to be chosen. I'd have backed out, but well. The murder. It's horribly tragic."

"So who would he have given the position to...?"

"Mr Bloom outranked me, but between you and me, he wasn't the most reliable of candidates. I don't think he'd have lasted long in the job."

He was probably right there.

"Did you speak to the other candidates?" I asked.

"No. Two of them got into a childish argument outside the interviewing room after we left," he said. "I don't want to impose on you, but I heard a rumour you've taken a particular interest in Mr Bayer's death, and the possibility one of your candidates was involved. Perhaps that's true, but there's another spellmaker in the town who might have an obvious reason to take out the competition. I'm not trying to point fingers, but both of them worked on similar spellcrafting methods. I was going to apply there next, actually."

"Oh." None of his words rang as untruthful to me. He'd answered all my questions. Almost too quickly, though maybe I was just still jumpy after the break-in. Whatever the reason, before I could question my better judgement, I found myself asking, "Did you murder Mr Bayer?"

His eyes widened. "No. Why would I?"

No lies. Great one there, Blair. "Sorry. Like I said—it's been a long day. Good luck with the new job."

He smiled at me, with no warmth this time, and walked out.

I remained in the interview seat and clapped slowly to myself. "Stellar job, Blair."

"Who are you talking to?" said Bethan, peering in.

I pressed a hand to my forehead. "Well, we can forget inviting him back. Where are the others?" She appeared to be the only person in the office.

"We've got the rest of the day off again," she said. "Three shifter healers couldn't turn Callie back into human form, and she accidentally knocked one of them out. Not her fault —she never was particularly good at coordinating herself while in shifted form. It's why she doesn't work for the pack."

"Oh no." I frowned. "What about the werewolves? Might they be able to ask her who attacked her and then tell us?"

"She's—well, she's had to be sedated, to be honest. The healers were really freaked out."

"Oh. Sorry. I guess we have to wait to find out who the intruder was."

Bethan nodded. "She probably won't shift back until she wakes up. The boss wants to check in on her at the hospital, so she's letting us go home instead."

What a week. Three disgruntled clients would probably never work with our company again, and I was even further from the killer than before. Which is where any sane person would want to be, but I was more annoyed than was probably wise. I'd been sure Simeon had been hiding something behind his polished appearance.

With no word from Callie and an afternoon free, I decided to go to the shops again. The break-in all but proved that the culprit was one of the interviewees, but maybe what Simeon had said held some merit. And to be honest, I was kind of curious as to what a spellmaker actually did.

Steve the gargoyle police chief, however, apparently had the same idea. I spotted his winged form ambling past and swiftly ducked into the nearest shop—a bookshop.

Towering shelves housed countless titles—all unfamiliar to me. I jumped when a book lifted itself off the shelf into the hands of a little green man beside me. Two witches stood giggling in the 'hexes and charms' section, while a moody-looking, pale man lurked in the history section. I stared for a moment, overwhelmed.

"What are you looking for?" asked the small green winged man at my side. "Can I help you?"

"Are you a fairy?" I asked stupidly.

"Leprechaun," he said. "You must be the new girl."

"That's me. I'm looking for something on... history. Town history."

"Oh, just ask around," he said cheerfully. "Otherwise, try asking Vincent over there." He indicated the moody-looking man in the corner. "He's lived here since the start."

The guy didn't look that old, from a distance. Vampire, then. "Sure, I'll ask him. Er, do you have any books on... spellmaking?"

"Not specialist ones. They're usually unique to the spellmaker. Pity Mr Bayer is gone—he used to make the best ones." He dropped his voice. "You're new here, so you probably don't know, but he died recently."

"I do. I mean, he was a client of ours."

"That's very sad."

It sounded like the guy was reasonably well-liked. "Are there other spellmakers in the town?"

"Yes, there's Ruther."

Simeon had mentioned another spellmaker. He'd insinuated that this Ruther might have felt Mr Bayer posed a threat to his business...

"Thanks," I said to him. "I think I'd like to have a look around the reference section."

"Absolutely," he said. "Tap the higher shelves to get the list."

Tap the higher shelves? He'd disappeared before I had the chance to ask what he meant. I scanned the shelves. Their labels glowed around the edges and were slightly raised, like buttons. I stood on tip-toe and pressed my finger against the nearest. A piece of parchment unfurled to floor level, listing titles. When I tapped one of them, it dropped from the shelf above me and landed in my hand. *Advanced Levitation Spells.* Maybe not.

How to return it to its former position? I pondered, then tapped the book's name on the list again and it rose up, returning to the shelf. A smile formed as I imagined having my own library. I doubted this one held the same titles you found in the normal world, but magic kept on surprising me.

Invigorated, I strode down the row of shelves, conjuring up books every time one of them caught my eye. There were beginners' guides to magic, but Alissa had already offered to loan me her own, and I was lacking in the spare cash department. The 'monsters' section was entirely empty of people, but thankfully none of the books looked particularly monstrous, even the encyclopaedia. I wondered if Nathan regularly consulted that. Wait, he wasn't a paranormal hunter anymore…

My hand paused on a title: *Guide to Fairies and Other Species.*

The word *species* made my heart sink in an unpleasant manner. Against my better judgement, I lifted the title from the shelf, and flipped open the book. On the first page was a list of descriptors for identifying a fairy. Pointed ears. Green skin. I reached up to tweak my own ear. Not pointed. Definitely not green. No wings. But that was the point, wasn't it? Rita had said I was *glamoured.* But I *felt* human.

I opened the book again, skimming through to look up the definition of the word *glamour.* According to the book, glamour was a type of fairy-specific disguise magic, very powerful, and could only be undone by another fairy. I skimmed through the pages, hoping that I'd find out there was a way to undo it, but found nothing.

Disappointment churned inside me. Even the books didn't have answers. I could ask the vampire about town history, but what I really wanted was *my* history. Who had put the glamour on me? Why would they want me not to know who I was? I'd long since accepted I'd probably never know my real parents, but the aching curiosity refused to be satiated, and each tantalising clue only made the ache worse.

Movement flickered in the corner of my eye and I lowered the book.

"Found something interesting?" asked a deep voice from behind me.

I dropped the book on my toe. "No. Yes. Ow." I reached to pick it up, my face flaming, and shoved the book onto the shelf, upside-down.

The look on Nathan's face bordered on amused. "You're supposed to pay for the books, not read them, but I won't tell on you," he said. "What are you reading?"

"Got curious," I said. "There are all sorts of paranormals here and I've been kind of overwhelmed by it all, so I decided to have a look at all the different types. I was going to check out werewolves next."

"Because of Callie? I heard she was attacked."

"We're not sure if she was or not." I edged closer to the shelf, glad that at least he hadn't caught me in the monster hunting section. Unfortunately, his gaze went right to the book that I'd hastily returned to the wrong spot.

"Fairies? Is that what you're interested in?"

"Nope," I said quickly. *Lie.*

I know it's a bloody lie, I told the voice in my head.

Without warning, my vision swam, and suddenly the floor was a lot closer than it'd been before. The only reason I hadn't executed a full-on face-plant was because Nathan grabbed me by the arm. *What was that?*

"Take it easy." He looked a little alarmed. "Do you need to sit down?"

"No, I just thought I'd like to see the tiles up close."

Another wave of dizziness hit, and I couldn't even appreciate that he hadn't let go of my arm yet. I chewed on the inside of my mouth to keep from spitting out another lie.

"Come with me." He pulled me upright, still gripping my arm as though afraid I'd keel over, and steered me past the shelves towards a small café area at the back.

The world righted itself when I sat opposite him in a wooden seat. Only then did I notice that every group of people in the café had turned in our direction at once then quickly looked away as though to hide their interest. It didn't take a genius to figure out why: Everyone else in the café seemed to be a couple.

"You might have mentioned this was the town's most popular hangout for coffee dates," I said out of the corner of my mouth as they returned to their own conversations.

"It also has the best firework cappuccino in town."

"That sounds like a fire hazard," I remarked, scanning the menu. The last thing I needed was more caffeine with the residual adrenaline jangling inside me. "When it says magical side effects, will I turn into a wolf or start levitating?"

"Not quite, but I think they're a bit much for newcomers. Tea?"

"I don't like tea. Or jam. Yes, I know I'm a traitor to all things English and should probably head to the nearest airport."

He laughed at that comment. "I'm not keen on it either."

I scanned the menu. I could try a different type of magical smoothie every day of the week and not get through them all. "Calming smoothie, large."

"Better to go with medium," he said. "A large one will put you to sleep."

I think I've had enough experience with the floor tiles. "Medium it is. Do we have to go over there to order?" I indicated the counter, where nobody seemed to be queuing.

"No, just tap what you'd like on the menu. I'll pay." He scattered some coins onto the table.

"Oh—thank you." The menu lit up in the same way the lists of titles did on the bookshelves. I touched my fingertip to the right smoothie, and an instant later, it appeared in front of me, while the coins beside Nathan vanished. Witchcraft at its finest. "So you're not working today? What're you here for?"

His own drink appeared before him. It looked like coffee, from where I sat. "Would you believe I don't spend all my time waiting for newcomers by the lake?"

"Given how much of a novelty I am, I'm taking a wild guess it's never happened before."

"No, I can't say it has. Certainly not to me. How are you liking the job, by the way?"

"Aside from the fact that my co-worker is stuck as a wolf, it's been great."

"And have you met Madame Grey yet? I heard you're an honorary coven member," he said.

"That'd be because I'm living with her granddaughter. The witches seem to think they can drag some magic out of me by sheer force. You know, yesterday they made me stand outside in the rain in case I turned out to be a weatherworker?"

"They tend to attract those with stormy temperaments."

"Very funny." So he did have a sense of humour. "I think I'd prefer invisibility, or…" *Don't say flying.*

I picked up the smoothie and took a tentative sip. Despite its odd purple colour, it tasted of apple juice.

"Do you like it here so far?" Nathan asked.

"Yes. Absolutely. I really feel I've found my… tribe." Let's omit the fact that said tribe were a whole *species* away from me. And I still hadn't told him I was a fairy. I certainly wouldn't be doing so with an audience, even if I didn't suspect that I matched the exact type of misbehaving paranormal he used to help apprehend.

"I'm glad. You had a rocky start, and I can't help feeling responsible for that," he said. "I apologise for how I spoke to you when we met."

"You let me cry on the floor."

"I don't own the floor."

"Does Madame Grey own that, too?"

"I assume that was a joke, but… Yes. Yes, she does."

Wow. Lucky she seemed to like me. And so did he, unless he just felt sorry for the newbie. "You didn't have to listen to my sob story. I appreciate it." I sipped my drink. "What's your supernatural power, anyway?"

He raised an eyebrow. "Me?"

"I assume it doesn't involve stabbing things with pointy objects, otherwise humans can do it."

His smile vanished. Oops. Great one, Blair.

"Sorry. Bad choice of topic?"

"There are several 'monsters' in this café, including a vampire who's likely listening to every word we're saying."

"Ah. Sorry."

"No need to apologise. Which other magic types have you been tested for?"

"Setting things on fire, levitating, disappearing… I'm pretty sure I'd have managed that by now." Like right now, for instance. "I don't think I'd do well with a hazardous power."

"All magic has the potential to be hazardous," he said.

No kidding. Look what'd happened to Mr Bayer.

I drank the last of my smoothie, glancing over my shoulder to see if the vampire was still here. I had far too many questions about the business of being a paranormal hunter, and was starting to wish I'd had a closer look in that section after all. How often did paranormals go bad? Everyone said it was rare, but it must be common enough that independent hunters were a necessity. Hmm.

There was a sudden, ghastly howl. My blood went cold.

"What is that?" I asked.

It sounded like…

"A werewolf."

I jumped to my feet and ran out of the cafe. Nobody else did. Maybe they were used to howling wolves, but that voice sounded awfully familiar. Callie.

Nathan caught up to me at the door. "I think your co-worker just woke up."

"It sounds like she's in pain!" I looked around frantically. "Where—?"

"The hospital." He opened the door and pointed down the road at a larger brick building on the corner. "That's where she's likely to be."

Of course—it'd slipped my mind that when they'd said healers, they'd meant Alissa and her colleagues at the hospital. The town was small enough that there was a single hospital for all the paranormals.

"My flatmate Alissa works there." I began to walk in that direction. "I can find my way home from there."

Some end to the date that definitely wasn't a date. But if Callie was in trouble, I couldn't help feeling partly responsible.

I reached the hospital and walked into a clean, wide entryway. It wasn't hard to tell where Callie must be. A crowd had grown in a waiting room on my right, all blond and huge and… staring at me.

10

I backed away from the werewolves, and a withered hand rested on my arm. I jumped, looking sideways at the woman sitting in the only vacant seat. She leaned forward and whispered in my ear, "I hear you're a seer, like me."

Her eyes shone eagerly, making me want to back away. She looked a few sandwiches short of a picnic, to say the least. Her hair was a purple bird's nest and looked like it hadn't been washed in decades, and a wand stuck out from behind her ear. I really hoped she couldn't cast spells using it from that angle.

"Not exactly," I said carefully. I'd have to seriously revise everything that came into my head before speaking it aloud if I didn't want a repeat of the bookshop incident.

"There was a witch who lived here once. I knew her," she said. "Uncanny ability, being able to see the essence of a person without seeing their face."

"Uh. I can't... exactly..." How did she know I could do that? I hadn't told her.

Thankfully, at that moment, Alissa came out of one of the rooms. "Blair?" she said. "What are you doing here?"

"I came to check on Callie. I heard her screaming from all the way down the road."

"She's fine. Just a little disorientated. Ava, you're not supposed to be out of the ward." She addressed the old seer, who gave me one last piercing look before shuffling away.

"Who's she? A coven leader?"

"Retired," she said. "Ignore everything she says. Old Ava lost her marbles before she lost her hair. She likes giving false prophecies to mess with people."

"So the bird's nest is a wig?"

"Yes, and the wand isn't real, don't worry. It's made of plastic."

A nurse poked her head out of the room, calling to Alissa. "I'll be back in a minute," she said, heading into the room again. Leaving me alone with the werewolves.

If not for my sixth sense telling me what they were, I might have mistaken them for one large, very handsome family. All were blond and Scandinavian-looking, and none were outwardly paranormal, but my sixth sense now snapped on without conscious thought. *Uncanny* was one way of putting it. *Bloody terrifying* was another. Some of those wolves looked even more intimidating than Steve the Gargoyle, and though they seemed to cover several generations, all were blond and looked about the same age. I'd never asked if werewolves aged, like vampires didn't. I should have brought a handbook, but I'd never thought to search the bookshop for *Paranormals for Dummies* either. I doubted one existed. Either you were born into the world and knew it, or you weren't. No middle ground.

I stiffened when one of the larger werewolves got to his feet, making his way towards me with determined strides. He was really, really tall, which hadn't been obvious when he'd been sitting down, and I'd unintentionally backed myself into a corner when I'd walked away from Ava.

"You're Callie's co-worker?"

"Yes, I am." There was no point in pretending otherwise, and not just because I didn't fancy being acquainted with the floor tiles here. Even if the hospital was a more appropriate place than the bookshop. "Is she okay?"

"Don't mock me," he growled. "I heard you were there when she was attacked."

"Attacked?" I echoed. "We don't know if that's what happened. She was at work alone and someone broke in. I guess she panicked."

"She didn't panic," he said. "Someone forced her to shift, and even the expert healers can't change her back." He spoke through gritted teeth. "Who did that to her?"

"I don't know," I said. "She can't seem to communicate it to us."

He gave me an accusing stare. "She's my daughter," he said. "If she's not turned back soon, then I might have to take action myself."

He stalked away. I released the breath I'd been holding. To my intense relief, Alissa came out of the room again before any of the others could accost me.

"He seems friendly," I said in a low voice.

"Oh, he normally is," she said. "But shifters get pretty overprotective of family."

I'd be angry if one of my family members had been turned into a wolf against their will, too. If I'd had family members, anyway. And maybe my nosiness *had* partly been responsible. But I hadn't exactly intended to end up on the bad side of two of the scariest people in town.

Did the pack even know about the illegal werewolf? I

didn't want an innocent person to get into trouble if I'd misjudged the situation. And Vaughn's hiding his true identity didn't seem to have any connection with the murder or the break-in, as far as I knew.

"Can she really not turn back?" I asked.

"Apparently not," she said. "I guess it must have been a really powerful spell. I'm leaving in ten minutes, anyway. I can meet you outside, okay?"

"Sure. I'll see you in a bit."

I walked out of the waiting room, wishing there was something I could do to help. Staying out of the werewolves' way was the smartest move, but—

A dark-haired, pale man glided out of the room in front of me. He seemed to move on fast-forward, or the world seemed to slide out of his way—maybe a bit of both. And when he looked at me, my breath caught. His face was oddly waxen, his expression still, yet eerily handsome. He wore a black suit—*to hide bloodstains*—and couldn't have looked more like a vampire if he'd walked right out of the blood donation section.

Wait. In fact, that was precisely where he'd walked out of. I hoped that meant he didn't need any more fresh blood. Also, he was the same vampire I'd seen in the bookshop, so he'd clearly walked here while Nathan and I had been in the café.

Vincent, the guy in the shop had said his name was—and that he was the person to speak to if I wanted to know about town history.

"So you're the new blood," he said, eying me with interest.

Hearing that turn of phrase from a vampire was less than reassuring to say the least. "Yes, I am. I saw you at the bookshop. Why hang out in the history section if you lived through it all?"

"My memory isn't what it used to be."

He looked hardly older than me. "Er... how old are you?"

"Seven hundred and thirty."

"Oh. Wow."

He took a step forward, making me aware of how freakishly still he'd been beforehand. "You have a familiar look."

"You knew my family?"

"I've met a great number of paranormals."

He might have met all my ancestors from the fifteenth century for all I knew. "So you've been here since the town first started?"

"Yes, I have."

Oh. Tossing caution aside, I asked, "So why is this place called Fairy Falls if there aren't any fairies living here? Shouldn't 'not-fairy-falls' be more appropriate?"

"Haven't you heard the story yet?"

"You can probably assume I haven't, considering I'm new here."

"They say the fairies founded this town and used to live underneath the waterfall," said the vampire. "But one day there was a storm, followed by a rockslide. When someone went to check on the fairies, they'd disappeared without a trace, never to be seen again."

"That's not an ending."

"It's an ending. Just not the type you perhaps expected." He looked me up and down, and I suddenly remembered I was talking to a vampire and became conscious of my exposed neck. I wished I'd worn a turtleneck jumper instead.

"Thanks for the story," I said, edging backwards. "I need to go and find..."

"Relax." He reached out a hand. "I saw you talking to the werewolves, and I wanted to offer you a chance to ally with the vampires, in the interests of fairness."

ELLE ADAMS

"Fairness?" I echoed.

"As I said. Here's my card."

The card was blood red, with his name printed on it in an elaborate font. *Oh no. What feud have I wandered into this time?*

Thankfully, Alissa reappeared at that moment, and the vampire disappeared so swiftly that he left a blurred imprint on my eyelids. I breathed out.

"What's that?" She indicated the card in my hand. "Oh no. Put it away before the wolves see."

"Why is it always werewolves versus vampires?" I whispered to Alissa.

"Because they're uncivilised," said the vampire, reappearing around the corner.

Alissa mouthed *vampires have enhanced hearing.* Oops. Wow, he moved fast.

"As though drinking others' blood is civilised," said one of the werewolves, walking towards us. His jaw was clenched, and if he was that huge in human form, I dreaded to see what his wolf form looked like.

"If either of you starts a fight here, I'm kicking you both out," Alissa said, in ringing tones. In that moment, she sounded so much like her grandmother that it didn't surprise me when the vampire dipped his head and vanished. The werewolf narrowed his eyes and backed away.

"Sorry about that," said Alissa, as we walked out. "I should have warned you how bloody sensitive they are."

"Who, the vampires or the werewolves?"

"The werewolves, mostly, considering how on edge they are about Callie. You don't want to be on their bad side, but the vamps seem to think of you as a potential ally, since you're new."

"No thanks." I'd prefer to stick with the witches. At least they didn't look at me like I was a tasty snack. "Are there just were*wolves*? Or other weres?"

"Mostly. A few werefoxes, some werehedgehogs, but they hibernate most of the time."

Right. "And werebadgers?"

"Them, too."

And I thought I'd surpassed my quota of weirdness. "I don't have to pick a side, right?"

"Not yet. It doesn't matter too much. Most people respect the vamps, and the weres are friends with just about everyone."

"But not each other."

"Pretty much. Werewolves are temperamental, and protective of their families," she said. "That's why they're so twitchy at the moment. As for the vampires... I wish you hadn't run into him."

"He did tell me some town history," I said. "What was he here for, blood donations?"

"Yep. There are stringent laws about biting people without their consent."

"Good," I said.

"Did he tell you the story of the town?" she asked.

"He did." If anything, I felt less satisfied than before. But really, what had I expected? Answers on my own history to fall out of the sky? Maybe my real parents had never come from this town at all. Maybe I'd been looking in the wrong place. "How's the situation with Callie?"

"She's being kept overnight. We've tried most cures, but we might have to look into bringing a specialist in."

My heart sank. "I didn't know it was permanent." Nor did it seem a good omen that the wolves seemed to blame me for her situation.

"It shouldn't be," she said consolingly. "The wolves will make a huge song and dance about it, but they'll get over it when she recovers. Until then, I'd stay away from them."

"Wise advice."

ELLE ADAMS

————

The following day brought a new list of potential clients, and no answers on the break-in. I'd spent the night tossing and turning and dreaming of wolves and vampires deciding whether or not to seduce or snack on me. Way too on the nose, subconscious.

I entered the office, and found Lizzie and Bethan standing over the coffee machine.

"I think I broke it," said Lizzie.

"You're only supposed to conjure up one motivational coffee at a time," Bethan said.

"You'd need two if you had to deal with Mr Falconer." She shuddered.

"Who's Mr Falconer?" I asked.

"Wand-maker," Lizzie said, tapping her wand against the coffee machine. "His assistants keep running off, if you ask me, but he won't admit it. Anyway, everyone knows he's an awful boss, so I had to listen to him complain for an hour yesterday about how nobody appreciates good wand-work these days." She turned to me. "His wands *are* special, but don't tell him that... he already thinks he's amazing anyway."

"So I have that to look forward to." Or not. Did fairies even get wands? "Is Callie still stuck as a wolf?"

"Unfortunately, yes," Bethan said. "She woke up, but was groggy and wouldn't talk to anyone."

"Or growl at them. Not that it isn't serious," I hastened to add. "Will she talk to the pack? Or is there a way to understand werewolf speak?"

"Not if she won't talk," Bethan said. "The werewolves are furious."

"Her father cornered me last night," I admitted. "He seems to blame *me* for it. But I don't know what kind of spells can turn someone into a wolf."

"He blames *you?*" Lizzie tapped the coffee machine again. Several paper cups materialised, one after another, and a jet of coffee shot across the room, splattering the wall. "Oh no."

Blythe's head popped up from behind the computer. "What *are* you doing?"

"Fixing the coffee machine." Lizzie swore under her breath. "It's easily confused."

"Didn't you *make* it?" said Bethan, shaking her head. "Honestly. Blair, I wouldn't touch it."

"Wasn't planning to." I'd have to get my motivational boost somewhere else. "If the pack decides we're to blame for Callie's situation, shouldn't we be looking into cures for whatever spell the intruder used on her? Wait, weren't there traces in the reception area?" I cast my mind back to when we'd tidied up after Callie had overturned the desk. All we'd found was spilt coffee and paperwork.

Spilt coffee. The poison that had killed Mr Bayer came to mind, and a shiver ran down my arms. I didn't know the paranormal world well enough to make an educated guess on whether something similar had occurred this time, but it did remind me that I hadn't really thought much about the cause of his death.

Bethan waved her wand at the coffee on the wall and it vanished. "Honestly. Techno-magic is useful, but temperamental... how's your call list today?"

"Surprisingly light," I said, picking up the papers. "My inbox isn't, but would the boss object if I made a non-work-related call? I was thinking of speaking to a spell expert who might know what spell was used on Callie. If the pack hasn't done so already."

"We make calls that aren't on the list all the time," said Bethan. "Anyway, what do you think Veronica spent yesterday doing? She's incredibly vexed about the break-in."

"Do you think one of the people we questioned did it?" I

asked. "Probably not the last guy, and he outright said he never murdered Mr Bayer either. Unless my lie detector is faulty. But I'm kind of lost on how it's possible to turn someone into a wolf. The wizard might have been able to do it, but Vaughn has more of a motive."

"Maybe he did it to stop her from giving him away."

"Makes sense, but he must have guessed *I* knew," I said. "Also, he's terrible at magic. So unless he used a potion... is that possible?"

"I'm not sure. I don't think I've ever seen a shifter change forms against their will before," Bethan said. "Unfortunately, in a place of magic, there are rather a lot of spells that can cause someone's nature to change, or transformations. And the fact that she's so far been unable to communicate her plight makes it tricky for us. No traces were left in the office."

"So—is it permanent?" My heart lurched.

"No, but it depends if there's a counter spell or not." She tapped her pen against the desk. "She was already a werewolf beforehand, so regular transformation spells wouldn't do a thing. Maybe a spell that encouraged her to return to her true nature, or something like that. It might be trickier to reverse that type of spell, but not impossible."

What would have happened if the witness hadn't been a werewolf? Would the intruder have done worse? It was starting to look like none of the suspects had a real motive, except perhaps the other werewolf. I still had my doubts. We were missing several clues, whether the intruder had been trying to sabotage the investigation or just scare us.

Either way, I doubted Steve the Gargoyle would go out of his way to help with this end of the investigation. And I had a plan of action of sorts. If it *was* a potion that'd turned Callie into a wolf, the owner of the local apothecary might be able to steer me in the right direction. I had a few questions to ask about the nature of magical poisons. Including, perhaps, how Mr Bayer had died.

11

One phone call later put me through to Mr Grant, the owner of the local apothecary. I'd debated speaking to the other spellmaker first, but that'd be a little too obvious. It might be a good idea to learn more about poisons first, too.

"Hello," I said. "I'm Blair, from Dritch & Co."

"The new girl."

Even he knew who I was? "Yeah, that's me."

My mind conjured up an image of a friendly-looking man with greying hair at his temples. I'd have to be careful with my cover story and little white lies this time if I didn't want to fall on my face again. Unless I took the phone call while lying on the floor, but somehow I doubted that would escape the boss's attention.

"What can I do for you?" he asked.

"One of my co-workers is a werewolf, and got stuck in wolf form," I told him. "At first we thought she shifted by accident, but now we suspect someone did it on purpose. Since we didn't find traces of a spell, I wondered if there's a potion or charm which can do that to a person."

"Is this about the girl? Callie?"

"Yes," I admitted. "We're getting pretty concerned. Since I'm not acquainted with the pack, I thought someone who has experience with those types of potions might be able to help."

"There *is* a potion called moonbane which imitates the effects of the moon cycle on werewolves, but it usually wears off after a few hours."

"Oh. It was longer than a few hours ago." So much for that theory. "Is there another way?"

"If there is, it's not my area. Sorry to say, potions and poisons are all I know about. Transformative spells are generally spellcraft-related."

"Did you know Mr Bayer?" I asked.

"I did. It's tragic, what happened to him." His words rang with sincerity. "I already gave my statement to the police. He never bought our herbs... he preferred to grow his own. Those poisons are not something I stock on my shelves. I have enough people coming in trying to buy ways to curse their enemies as it is."

My lie-sensor didn't go off. He was telling the truth. "Okay. Just curious. Would a spellmaker know about spells that can trap someone in wolf form? Like the other one, Mr Ruther?"

"Maybe," he said. "He and I haven't spoken recently."

"You know him?"

"Personally? No. We've passed one another on the street a few times. I heard he hired a new assistant and handed most of the work over to him, since he's close to retirement, but other than that, I have no idea what he's currently working on."

If he'd hired an assistant, then he might have used Dritch & Co's services. "Thank you," I said.

After I hung up, I turned to Bethan. I'd been so absorbed

in the call that I hadn't registered her usual frantic style of juggling seven tasks at once. She looked up at me with a pen between her teeth and three others sticking out of her hair. "Any answers?"

"Not a potion," I said, suddenly feeling bad for leaving her to hold the fort alone. "Did you or one of the others help Mr Ruther find an assistant six months ago?"

"I think Blythe handled that one."

Of course she did. "Might you be able to get hold of the contact details?"

She tilted her head. "What are you scheming this time?"

"Spellmakers," I said. "I spoke to the apothecary's owner, and he claims that Callie wasn't affected by a potion. That means it was a spell. Apparently, Mr Ruther's assistant more or less runs the spellmaker's place now."

"And it has nothing to do with the murder."

"No clue. If it did, it'd solve a few problems at once, right?"

"And possibly create new ones." She tapped the mouse on her computer. "Head's up, Lizzie—"

The printer growled and spat a sheet of paper directly at me. It hit me full in the face, nearly knocking me out of my seat. "Whoa. Someone's in a mood."

"Someone disapproves of whatever you're scheming," Lizzie said from the other side of the desk.

Ow. I retrieved the sheet of paper, rubbing my nose. How did one make it up with a printer? I'd always thought technology hated me, but this was on a whole new level. I checked the assistant's number. Maybe I was better off calling him outside of work hours.

"Watch out," Bethan muttered. "Boss incoming."

I hid the printed sheet under the other files on the desk and casually turned to my emails instead. Not wanting to push my luck, I put my plans firmly in the back of my head as the door opened.

"Callie is back," said Veronica, striding into the office. "We've put her on guard duty. To scare off any more intruders."

"Has she spoken to anyone yet?" I asked.

"Apparently she doesn't remember the attack," she said. "I persuaded the pack—or more specifically, her father—to let her come back to work. She can identify the intruder if they decide to come in here again."

Good idea. If I invited the candidates back in for another interview, then Callie might be able to identify her attacker. Assuming I could come up with a convincing excuse.

I tried calling the spellmaker during my lunch hour, but the calls went through to voicemail. If Mr Grant was right, the assistant was running the show, so maybe he'd answer his own phone instead. I had fifteen minutes of my lunch break remaining, so I'd better make them count. I dialled the assistant's number and hoped Blythe hadn't left such a terrible impression on the candidate that he never wanted to work with us again.

"Hello," I said. "Is this Leopold, Mr Ruther's assistant? I'm sorry to bother you. This is Blair, from Dritch & Co recruitment."

"Oh hello," he said. My mind projected the image of a young man grinning at the phone. "I never did thank you properly for getting me the position. Wait—did you say Blythe?"

"No, Blair. I'm new," I said. So she'd apparently been nice to at least *one* person. "I wanted to ask you a couple of questions. We had an incident with a spell in our office, and..."

"And the man himself left his phone turned off. Tell me how I know." He laughed.

"I don't suppose you know how one would go about

turning someone into a werewolf? I mean, someone who's already a werewolf." I really should have written a script before making the call.

"Oh, Callie."

Did everyone know? Maybe my hopes that my notoriety as a newbie would fade were doomed to remain unfulfilled. "Yeah. It wasn't a potion. We've worked that much out. I figured the resident spellmaker would know."

"Hmm. They might have used a custom-made spell, but I'd be more inclined to say the caster was there in person and used a wand."

"I don't suppose there's a way to track who cast a spell?" I asked.

"Not unless they left their wand behind."

"Isn't there a reverse spell?"

"If it was done with a wand, only the caster can reverse it," he said.

No wonder the other werewolves were so ticked off. "She's been stuck like that for two days and I think her dad wants to strangle me. Is there nothing I can do?"

"Let me help you," he said, his tone changing entirely. "I heard you're new to magic, right? I can give you some pointers. Would you like that?"

I might be oblivious at the best of times, but I knew when someone was flirting with me. I knew so little about the temperament of his employer that this seemed an innocent way to get information out of him. It wasn't such a terrible thing to consider taking him up on his offer, right?

"Let me get back to you on that," I said. "I just wondered, though—you applied to work for Mr Ruther six months ago. Did you apply to work for Mr Bayer as well?"

"No, his last assistant was still working for him at the time. Clare."

Hmm. "Where is she now?"

"Now? Working at the Laughing Pixie. You know, the pub. Tell you what—want to meet there tomorrow night?"

I should say no. And yet. "Sure."

His flirtatious smile was back. "I can meet you there."

I looked at my phone, shaking my head and glad he couldn't see *my* expression. At least meeting an overeager spellmaker apprentice for a date was slightly less hazardous than speaking to the werewolves' grumpy leader or running into Steve the Gargoyle.

I returned to work. But today had reminded me that I hadn't addressed the obvious and spoken to people who'd actually known the victim. The attack on the office had diverted my attention, and by now, I was thoroughly encroaching on the police's territory. And yet—the spell on Callie was all but permanent. What if the killer targeted one of us next?

———

With the boss hovering over our shoulders all afternoon, we finished our work in record time. Feeling restless after an afternoon in the office, I walked the short distance to the shops, my thoughts churning. Before I knew it, my feet had carried me right up to Mr Bayer's place again. I peered up at the interview room, wishing I had a spell to unlock doors or even levitate myself up to the top floor. Wings would come in handy. Would the rest of my powers appear as suddenly as my ability to sense lies, or was that the only magic I'd ever get? I stood on tip-toe, almost able to see inside… wait, there was a narrow alley between the shop and its neighbour, and the wooden door leading through was already open. I might get a better view from around the back.

Trespassing now? I ignored the warning voice in my head and slipped down the alley. The wooden door was unlocked, suggesting someone had already checked the back garden. *I'll just have a look.*

I passed through the gate and peered over the low fence into the overgrown garden. The poisoned plant had come from in there, but I didn't see anything but weeds. I'd looked the picture of the plant up in the basic witchcraft guide Alissa had loaned me. A large plant with pink-patterned leaves. I wouldn't have a hope of identifying it amongst the tangled mass of weeds over the fence. Hadn't he only died last week? Unless magical plants grew quicker than regular ones, the garden sure seemed to have grown out of hand quickly. Of course, he might have kept it that way deliberately to ward off potential trespassers.

I looked past the plants towards the back window of the shop, but saw nothing. If the garden had been in this state last week, nobody could have easily sneaked in the back way. That meant the killer had come in from the front, or had already been there. Which I'd suspected already, but if they'd poisoned him with his own plants, they'd have needed access to the garden, right?

I moved right up to the fence, looking for pink-veined leaves, and jumped violently when a pair of teeth snapped inches from my face. A man-sized plant that alarmingly resembled a Venus flytrap leaned over the fence, its mouth big enough to swallow a person.

I backed away, spotting identical plants growing around the outskirts of the garden.

Okay. They definitely didn't go in the back way, then. Or climb the fence, either. I backed carefully down the alley. *This is a bad idea.*

There was a blinding flare of light, followed by a muffled explosion—and the ground gave way. A startled scream escaped me as stone became mud and kept sliding, a deep trench forming in the earth where the alley had been. My feet skidded uncontrollably—right towards the gaping mouths of the monstrous plants.

I'm going to die.

I threw up my hands.

My feet stopped skidding and abruptly left the ground. I gasped, my body trembling, my vision blurring. Was I *flying?*

I blinked, my vision clearing. I stood at the entrance to the alley, my feet firmly on solid ground once again. An odd tingling passed over my shoulder blades. I released a breath, staring at the alley. The trench in the earth had entirely disappeared, and the alley looked exactly the same as before. But I was certain I'd been seconds from being swallowed up by a troop of deadly Venus flytraps. *They* were still there, long feelers drooping over the fence, heads moving as though they could sense my presence. Intelligent killer plants. And to think everyone had labelled Mr Bayer as kindly and well-mannered. Deadly plants were just the trick to keeping people's hands off his property, but they didn't give me any more answers about the murder.

Speaking of murder… I was ninety percent certain that someone had tried to kill me. I'd used some kind of magic, yet if not for the mud splattering my clothes, I'd have thought I'd imagined the whole thing. *What did I do?*

I backed out of the alley and all but ran home, my thoughts spinning. My memory was a blur, but I was so sure I'd—flown.

As I unlocked the door with shaking hands, Alissa gasped from behind me. "What happened to you?"

"Long story. I need a shower." I walked into the hall, kicking off my muddied shoes. I wouldn't be able to wear them for work tomorrow in that state, but that was the least of my worries. "Sorry—I'm dripping mud everywhere."

"A quick spell will take care of it," she said, dropping off her bag. "What did you do, go for a swim in the lake?"

I explained the situation, while she fed the cat. Roald eyed me suspiciously as though he could smell angry killer plants on me.

"You went to Mr Bayer's *garden?*"

"I know it was a stupid idea," I said, running a hand through my tangled hair. "I hardly expected someone to booby trap the place."

"Yeah, that sounds like a spell. Maybe one of Mr Bayer's own. *Dangerous,* though. You could get arrested for that if someone innocent got caught in the spell. I wouldn't have thought it was his type of thing."

I shook my head. "It was set up to stop me from getting into the garden. But those killer plants were enough of a deterrent of their own. I was looking for the poisonous leaves—but the person who killed him must have got them out of the garden, right?"

"Maybe he did it himself," she said, frowning. "But you have a good point. Have you told the police?"

"The gargoyle bit my head off the last time he caught me near there," I said. "I shouldn't have gone, I know."

"You used magic, though?"

"I have no idea what I did. Maybe I flew." I ran a hand over my shoulder blades, but they were definitely human. Not a wing in sight.

Her eyes rounded with understanding. "Wow. You should tell Madame Grey... I know you don't want to get into trouble, but this should be reported. You might have died."

"I know, but Steve has it in for me, and he'll know I wasn't there by coincidence."

She ran her teeth over her lower lip. "I know, but if you end up getting hurt, and we didn't tell anyone..."

"Steve will probably say it's my own fault anyway. I shouldn't have gone nosing around there in the first place. Anyway, I need to get this mud off me."

It took half an hour of scrubbing to get the mud off and my nails were a disaster, not to mention my hair. Clean and relatively dry, I headed back into the living room to find Alissa had made me a mug of a witch remedy designed to calm the body and mind. I sipped the spiced drink, sighing as the warmth went right to the tips of my toes. It'd been years since I'd spent any substantial amount of time with my other friends since they'd all paired off. It was nice to just enjoy one another's company.

"You don't have to talk about the case now," she said. "But I'd like to know how you ended up in that alley to begin with. You learned something new, right?"

I briefly explained today's phone calls.

"So Callie is stuck like that indefinitely?"

"Until we find who put the spell on her," I said. "We're still at a dead end with that one. I guess the only option left is to talk to the other werewolves, if she's coherent enough for them to understand. But considering their leader seems to hate me…"

"There are others," said Alissa, petting Roald. "Not all of them would blame you. I think only the leader of the pack does, and that's because Callie's his daughter. There's the pack beta…"

"But…?" I prompted.

"But he's my ex." She grimaced. "I don't mind going with you to the New Moon. It's the most popular hangout for weres, and he'll be there tomorrow night, for certain. All the weres like to go there to blow off steam, and you haven't met the other shifters yet."

"Are you sure?" I said. "I'm supposed to be meeting Leopold at the Laughing Pixie tomorrow, too."

"Wait, the spellmaker's assistant?"

"Leopold? Yeah, he offered to introduce me to Mr Bayer's former assistant."

Her brows rose. "On a date?"

"No. Well, maybe he thinks it is. It's the quickest way to get information." It'd be even better if I had any skill whatsoever in the flirtation department.

She grinned. "Fair warning, that co-worker of yours is telling everyone about seeing you on a date with Nathan yesterday. You didn't mention that."

I groaned, heat creeping up my neck. "It wasn't a date. I was checking out the bookshop. How did she even know that? Wait, don't tell me. She's been rifling through people's thoughts again." Specifically, mine. Shouldn't there be a law against that? It sounded like the paranormal world was strongly regulated, so it made little sense for someone to walk around with the ability to pull someone's thoughts out of their head whenever they wanted to.

"She wasn't the only witness," said Alissa. "The description specifically involved the word 'swooning'."

I groaned again. "Not even close. Turns out I can't lie without falling over now."

She blinked. "You—can't lie at all?"

"As of yesterday, apparently," I said. "Which is going to prove problematic at work considering the boss doesn't know I'm a fairy and neither does half the town."

Veronica had been on the warpath today, which had made me reluctant to start anything. According to Bethan, she'd worked on upping security at our workplace. You'd think a retired paranormal hunter would be enough, though. What type of magic was he hiding? It was none of my business, whether we'd gone to a popular coffee date hangout or not. He was cute, but probably unavailable. It didn't sound like he had a girlfriend at least, and he had insisted on paying for my drink. But so had a dozen people on my first night.

"Hmm," she said. "I've never heard of a spell stopping someone from lying before, but I can't say I'm an expert on fairies. I probably wouldn't draw attention to it, not with the rumours about Callie."

"Let me guess: Blythe is blaming that one on me, too."

"You've got it. Sorry. If it's any consolation, she'll have forgotten once the whole case is cleared up, and so will everyone else."

"Not soon enough. I'm pretty sure at least a dozen people saw me running back here covered in mud."

"At least you didn't run into Nathan again."

"Don't even. I doubt anyone would have tried to kill me with the town's resident paranormal hunter around anyway."

That thought sobered me up. I'd had a close call, not to mention I'd left a muddy trail all the way down the high street. I hoped it didn't mean the killer could follow me home. Not that I'd actually seen anyone else near the place—but who'd set up the trap?

The killer had covered their tracks. Maybe what I needed was a more direct approach after all. It wasn't like I had no paranormal powers of my own.

12

I more or less worked on autopilot throughout Friday, anticipating my interviews that evening. Not that the interviewees in question knew I planned to question them. Small wonder that I almost forgot about my first magical theory lesson with Rita after work. I hurried to the witches' headquarters to find her already leaving.

"There you are," she said. "Are you certain you want to do this today? I know you've had a rough week."

"I do," I said. "Sorry, I lost track of time. Is there a set theme for the lesson? I wasn't sure whether to bring anything or not."

"Since you're not on an official curriculum, I thought I'd let you choose the theme."

I followed her into the classroom she'd reserved for me, and took a seat in the front row. "That'd be great." Where to start? There were a hundred magical topics I wanted to know about. "I'm kind of lost on which types of talents are specialities and which can be learned by everyone. Can you give me a crash course in that?"

"I can," she said, conjuring a book to her hand. "Primary talents don't require a prop like a wand. They also can't be learnt by anyone outside of the bloodline, but it's possible to find other spells to act as a substitute. For instance, there are truth-sensing spells which would have effects similar to your own ability, but would likely not be as powerful or immediate. Each witch or wizard has only one primary skill, but it's generally their strongest."

Unless they drew the short straw and got stuck with a disappointing primary power. That must suck.

I listened patiently as she explained the different types of magic. Since primary skills ran in bloodlines, I wouldn't discover any others—but that was if I assumed fairy magic worked in the same way. It might not. Either way, other skills like potion-making, spells, curses and hexes were more universal. However, most spells could only be cast on the spot. It was much harder to trap them into the form of a potion or charm. What Mr Bayer did was unusual, and he had to be careful not to stray outside the boundaries of the magical laws. Aside from the killer plants, apparently.

"The most illegal spells are those which rob someone of their own free will," she explained. "Nasty magic."

"What about mind-reading?" I asked. "That seems invasive, to say the least."

"Latent powers don't count," she said. "Mind-readers are usually only good at that one thing. Nothing else. There's also a limit. The person has to be within a certain distance. A few feet, I think. It varies."

So Blythe talked a bigger game than she demonstrated. Good to know.

"Can it be blocked?" I asked.

"Funny you should ask that," she said. "I heard a rumour Mr Bayer was working on a type of handmade magical shield before he died. It's something nobody has yet been able to crack. Mind magic is out of the realms of study, because nobody aside from its practitioners knows how it works. It's also not the type of magic which has an everyday equivalent. You can't use a wand to suddenly give someone mind-reading abilities."

"Oh." I nodded. "That makes sense. Was Mr Bayer interested in that type of magic?"

"I don't think there was a single type of magic he *wasn't* interested in."

"Did you know him?"

"Not well, no. He kept to himself. Is there anything else you'd like to know?"

"You mentioned distance being a factor with mind-reading. Is it the same for all powers?" I'd yet to test the limits of my own ability. What with it being an unknown, I might even be the first to know.

"Distance?" she echoed. "I can't wave my wand and levitate something on the other side of town, if that's what you mean. Magic gets harder the further the distance, but it's possible to get around that with studying." She waved her wand in demonstration, knocking the door into the main hall open. "I can probably go as far as the end of the hall, provided there isn't anything in the way. But witches and wizards can't cast spells through solid objects, including windows. Does that answer your question?"

"It does. Thank you. Is spellmaking seriously advanced magic? Can anyone learn it?"

"Only if apprenticed to a master," she said.

Hmm. Odds were, whoever had set up that magical trap had stolen it from Mr Bayer... or he'd set it up himself. But surely someone would have noticed if he was making illegal and dangerous spells.

"Something on your mind?" she asked.

I debated, then asked, "I was wondering—is there a homemade spell that can make the ground collapse?"

"There's a spell for almost everything. Skill is another matter entirely."

Skill… that ruled out at least two of the candidates I'd questioned, and the third knew the least about my attempts at an investigation since our discussion had been brief. He'd also outright said he wasn't the killer, and I hadn't picked up on any lies. "Is it legal to set up a booby trap to throw someone into a pit?"

She arched a brow. "Didn't you hear the rules? It's highly illegal to use any kind of magic to do harm."

Then it wasn't Mr Bayer. It couldn't have been. Someone else had blocked the way into the garden. Unless he wasn't as benign as he'd appeared to everyone else in the town.

She returned to her lecture. I did my best to take it all in, but my mind kept wandering over to the suspects, and poor Callie. I was certain I'd missed something, but my magical knowledge was limited to say the least. My two unexpected talents didn't make up for a lifetime of studying. Maybe I was best leaving the case to the experts, but Steve the Gargoyle didn't strike me as someone who knew the nuances of magical traps, either. Evidently *he* hadn't checked the back garden…

After I left work that evening, I'd got halfway home before I remembered my date. No time to change, so I hoped my casual skirt and top would do. I made my way to the Laughing Pixie, and entered the bustling pub.

It was lucky that I'd already 'seen' what Leopold looked like, otherwise I'd never have been able to pick him out of the crowd of witches and wizards. I scanned the cramped space and spotted him at a table by the window. The rest of the pub was packed out with young student-aged people chatting and laughing.

"Hey, Blair." He stood, smiling blindingly. "Glad you could make it."

I took a seat. "Is Clare here?"

"She's working on the bar. Hey, Clare!" He waved frantically, drawing attention to the fact that my sensing abilities had neglected to inform me that he was younger than me. Thankfully not a teenager, but maybe twenty-one or so. I'd had enough trouble connecting with student-aged people when I *was* one, let alone now.

A girl with spiky hair ambled over, spitting on a cloth then using it to clean the glass in her hand. I made a mental note to figure out how to cast a germ-repelling charm or never come here again.

"*You* used to be Mr Bayer's apprentice?" Oops. I probably should have attempted to hide my surprise.

She blinked. "Yeah. Why?"

"I work for the recruitment firm Mr Bayer used to hire you," I explained. "You're a qualified witch?"

"Yeah, but I didn't help with spells. Just cleaning the lab, and background work. I left because he decided he wanted someone to help with the actual spellmaking. I'm not great at it."

"Was he easy to work with?"

"Easy? Sure. He wasn't mean or anything. Overprotective of his spells, though."

"Did you ever see what he was working on? I guess you wouldn't have been allowed into his lab or anything, right?"

She wiped her nose on the cloth. Yeuch. "Yeah, of course I was. I was the one who cleaned up after him. The only place I wasn't allowed to go was the garden."

And there was my opening. "I heard he has some interesting plants there."

"Those horrible things?" She wrinkled her nose. "I imagine they're running wild now."

You might say that. "Is it legal to have trained security plants?"

"They were trained not to attack unless someone trespassed. Wait, who told you that anyway?"

"I met a lot of people on my first night here," I said evasively. "I heard a lot of rumours, too. Just got curious about him."

I didn't have to outright lie, and evasions apparently weren't bad enough to trigger any side effects. One problem solved.

"It sounds weirdly paranoid, though," I added. "Did he think he was going to get attacked?"

"No, he thought someone was going to steal his supplies. Nobody made spells like he did. His shop was covered in defences that would alert him if there was an intruder, too. Nobody could get in."

As a former employee, she'd have had access, but she sounded genuine, and she hadn't lied.

"So he thought someone might steal his ideas?" I asked. "Another spellmaker?"

"I wouldn't have thought so," she said. "He kept on about how the others had no imagination. He wanted to make *real* defensive spells. I guess it was his undoing in the end, 'cause he never told anyone his secrets."

"Not you?"

She shook her head. "Not the actual spell recipes. All I did was clean up after him."

Hmm. It didn't sound like there was a rivalry going on—on Mr Bayer's part, at least.

"Did he tick anyone off lately?" I asked.

"No," she said. "He was mostly a loner and didn't talk about work outside of the shop. Family's gone... he had a few friends, but he went out of his way not to antagonise anyone. Sold to everyone. Even werewolves."

"Is it that much of a big deal that the paranormals don't intermingle? I mean, the werewolves and vamps?"

"No," Leopold cut in. "Aren't you going to take our orders?"

She gave a startled blink. Oops. I'd momentarily forgotten that he'd thought we were on a date. And I'd got all the information I needed. I wouldn't be drinking so much as a sip from one of these filthy glasses.

"I'm sorry." I got to my feet. "I remembered I have to meet a friend soon."

His expression drooped. "Seriously?"

"Seriously," I said. "Thank you for your time," I added to Clare.

Leopold's face reddened. "You didn't even want to talk to me, did you?"

Guilty. In fairness, he'd dangled the bait himself. "Look, I'll level with you. Mr Bayer's killer attacked one of my colleagues and I'm looking for all the leads I can get. Sorry I deceived you."

Gathering what was left of my dignity, I half ran from the pub, remembered I hadn't asked Alissa for directions, and walked the wrong way three times before finding the right street.

Once I'd found the street, it wasn't hard to locate the New Moon, the werewolves' favoured local pub. The sounds of a guitar being strummed inexpertly grated on my eardrums, followed by a drumbeat that sounded like someone dropping a stack of heavy textbooks down a flight of stairs. I didn't see Alissa, so I found a free table as far from the stage as humanly possible and ordered one of the cocktails I'd liked before—after checking the glasses were clean, that is.

"Hey," said Alissa, sitting down opposite me. "I should have warned you they have live music on a Friday night."

"Calling that music is stretching the definition a little." I rubbed my forehead. "I don't suppose there's a cocktail that temporarily makes me unable to hear loud noises?"

"Unfortunately not," she said. "They haven't improved much."

"Wait. Is one of those people the guy I'm meant to be meeting?"

"You've got it. Bryan's one of the only members left from the original band. He used to make me go to his live shows for moral support."

Her ex either wore thick earplugs or his enhanced were-wolf senses somehow warped the racket coming from the stage into actual music.

"Which is he?"

"The guy playing the guitar. Yes, I did put an earplug charm on myself, and we broke up after he found out."

I winced. "Do we have to wait until they've finished playing before we can speak to them?"

"Yep. Want to get some food? My treat. You shouldn't have to pay to listen to this."

I had to agree with her there. We ate and sipped our drinks while waiting for the never-ending set to draw to a close. Nobody asked for an encore, but they got three anyway. Despite the cocktails, my energy was flagging. When a table closer to the stage cleared, Alissa and I moved there.

"Thank you for listening!" the lead singer howled into the microphone. "And now for the final encore!"

A quiet groan rose up from the corner, where the other patrons had started some sort of game. At first, I thought they were playing at pool tables, but the balls appeared to be floating around, as the patrons tapped them with wands.

The wolves didn't seem to sense their audience's lack of

enthusiasm, because they launched into an energetic number that was the musical equivalent of a brick being thrown around in a washing machine. I was on the verge of walking away when the song finally drew to a close, and the band traipsed off the stage to lukewarm applause.

The guitarist spotted Alissa right away, and sidled up to our table. Like the other werewolves, he was huge and muscular. Attractive, I supposed, but after hearing him playing the guitar, I'd be keeping my distance.

He bared his teeth at her. "You look great."

"Thanks," she said.

"What did you think of the set?"

"It was… different."

"Excuse me," I interrupted, before he could unintentionally force me to lie again. "We're actually here because I'd like to speak to you."

"You're Blair, right?" he said, eyeing me with interest.

"Yeah. I'm new here," I said. "I don't know if you've heard yet, but my co-worker is a pack member and is—well, kind of stuck in wolf form."

"Oh, Callie," he said. "I sometimes want to do that myself. Run away into the forest, away from all responsibilities…" He leaned on the table, and it was difficult to say if his leer was directed at me or Alissa.

"She's trapped," I said, annoyed at his dismissiveness. "Have you ever dealt with a situation like that before?"

"I don't know. Ask a witch. Alissa, want to come for a drink?"

"No, she doesn't," I said.

"You?"

I nearly threw the drink in his face. "No, I have one right here."

"Then I'll join you." He pulled out a chair.

"We're leaving, unless there's someone else in the pack

who can tell us if it's possible to reverse the spell on Callie," I said. "That's all we're here for."

He shrugged. "Your loss."

Another werewolf, a huge blond guy, appeared behind him. "You're Blair?"

"I am." I didn't think I'd met him, but he looked similar to the blond crowd at the hospital. Oh no. "I just wanted to know if Callie's spoken to any of you yet. That's all."

The werewolf got right in my face. "I heard you went on a date with the hunter."

"Excuse me?"

"Did you?"

"No, I didn't. Does it matter?"

"It matters because he's a murdering scumbag."

Whoa. "Whatever issue you have with him, has nothing to do with Callie. I wanted to know if she's spoken to any of you yet. That's all."

He looked at me like I was out of my mind. "No. You need to mind your own business, newbie."

"She's my co-worker," I said, in my best 'reasonable' tone. "Our office was attacked. If we find out who cast the spell on her, then we can reverse it, and we'll have caught the intruder, too. I like Callie and I don't want her to be stuck like that forever. And I don't want the burglar to go after my friends, either."

He leaned over. "Not my problem. Leave Callie and the pack alone, human."

And he stormed off.

"Sorry about him," said Alissa, in a low voice. "I knew the pack leader wouldn't be here, but I forgot the others might not like that you were on a date with Nathan."

I groaned. "It wasn't a date by any stretch of the imagination. I nearly passed out on a shop floor and he felt sorry for me. Are the other paranormals going to come after me or shun me because of him?"

"Only rival suitors, maybe." She grinned. "I'm joking. But I'd cheer you on."

"You're not going to drop this, are you?"

Her eyes glittered with amusement. "See how you feel when it's not so overwhelming."

"Or if I feel it's worth making enemies over," I said. "Does the whole pack hate the paranormal hunters?"

It didn't sound like the type of profession one went into to make friends, but if I spent any more time with Nathan, would it turn the other townspeople against me?

"No, not the whole pack. Only people who have a personal issue with him, I guess."

It sounded that way, from how that werewolf spoke. But he and Callie seemed to get on fine. "He's not a paranormal in the usual sense, right? I mean, he's not a witch, or a shifter, clearly. Or a fairy."

She snorted. "Nope. I'm trying to work out how to explain... there are a certain number of humans—not many —who are born with the second sight but no magical powers. They can see us and interact with us, but have no magic of their own."

"Has he made enemies in all the paranormal groups, then?"

"Enemies? Not at all. The wolves don't *like* hunters, but most of them aren't petty enough to carry a grudge. The other paranormals don't care. He's one of us."

"Because every unattached woman wants to score with him? That's the impression I'm getting."

"No. I mean, yes, but you've seen the competition." She gestured at the stage, and I shuddered. "Anyway, it sounds like he likes you."

I shrugged. "Maybe. See if the novelty wears off first.

Clumsiness is an endearing trait until you have to live with it. He's probably put me in the 'hazard' category by now."

"I think that spot's reserved for the monsters, to be honest."

"Ha." I smiled, unable to help myself. Never mind Nathan —it was refreshing to have a friend to hang out with.

Even if the werewolves did start up another rendition of some horrible ballad. We took that as our cue to leave.

13

I woke up bright and early on my first weekend in Fairy Falls, with Roald the cat licking my ear. I didn't even scream this time, instead reaching to pet him. "You and I are going to have to talk about personal space at some point, Mister."

The cat rubbed against my head, making my hair turn static. I yawned and sat up, dislodging him as carefully as I could manage, and looked out at the bright gardens. My first order of business for today ought to be to finally connect my phone to the paranormal network. Hopefully I'd be able to call and check on my foster parents. Not to mention my friends. For all I knew, my phone was blowing up with messages while my signal remained absent. If Rebecca wanted a babysitter this weekend, she was out of luck. The only reason I hadn't gone broke in my weeks of unemployment was due to her paying me double to watch her adventurous three-year-old and cantankerous one-year-old. I was even less good with children than I was with animals, but I'd been desperate.

Life had changed so much in a week. It bothered me a

little how quickly I'd adapted, but I'd had to. Besides, home had always been a temporary state for me, not permanent. Maybe it came from not knowing who I really was.

I found Alissa in the kitchen. "Any plans today?" she asked.

I stuck some bread in the toaster. "Grocery shopping. Laundry. Don't they have spells for that?"

"They do," she said. "But Madame Grey doesn't like to encourage laziness."

"I call it practicality," I said. "I don't even have my bank card or phone properly set up."

She slapped a hand to her forehead. "Right—I can help you do that first. I forgot you have to sign up in person. I got signed up at birth like everyone else."

"Story of my life," I said. "I always thought there was a handbook of life skills I missed out on somewhere."

She laughed. "You'll learn in time. As for shopping, you know you can order a delivery, right?"

"I didn't know you used delivery companies here." I should know better by now. This was the twenty-first century, magical or not.

"We've lived alongside normals for long enough to mimic their ideas," she said.

"Occasionally we have good ones."

After breakfast, we walked to the town centre, where Alissa led me to the bank and helped me fill out their forms. Magic sped up the process, and within minutes I had my bank account all set up. Then we stopped at the phone shop and connected my mobile to the paranormal network on a plan which would allow me to call and message people outside of the town.

"So," Alissa said, "now the boring part is out of the way, do you want to go and buy some serious mud-proof shoes in case of any more mishaps?"

"Maybe I'd be better off getting a levitating suit of armour covered in bubble wrap."

She laughed. "Hey—levitation. I have an idea."

She all but pulled me into a shoe shop. I'd always hated shoe shopping, but magical shoes ranged from waterproof mermaid-tails to ones which changed your appearance. Alissa pointed eagerly at a display of new releases.

"Seven Millimetre Boots?" I said dubiously.

"Seven League Boots got outlawed because people kept ending up lost at sea," she explained, kicking off her own shoe. She pulled the boot on and took a deliberate step forward. The boot zipped forwards... well, seven millimetres.

"Isn't that just... one step?" I said dubiously.

"In any direction." She stepped *up,* leaving the ground. "See?"

I had to admit that was kind of cool.

"Seven each way." She stepped up, walking in a zigzag pattern on the air. "You can keep going. It's more stable than a flying carpet or broomstick, or even a plain old levitation spell."

"I've never seen a flying carpet or broomstick."

"That'd be because they only fly on clear days. Health and safety nightmare otherwise."

"Like skydiving."

"You've done that?"

I took the boot she offered me. "No way, but I'd trust a professional with a parachute more than I trust my ability to control a stick of wood a mile up in the air. I think I'll take the boots instead." I slipped my foot into it, and to my surprise, it fit. Either the two of us were the exact same shoe size or the shoes magically resized themselves. Now *that* would make shopping less tedious.

"It's lucky you're too old for the witch academy," she said.

"But they make the parents sign a hundred forms before sending them out to fly."

"Hogwarts didn't seem to do health and safety warnings," I observed, slipping my other foot into the second boot. "How can you live here and not have read Harry Potter?"

She shrugged. "Why read fantasy when you live it?"

"That's not all it is." I smiled. "I'll convince you. Watch and see."

"I have a feeling you're going to win that argument. Anyway, try the boots."

I did. My feet zipped upwards, then again. *Whoa.* I took another few steps, then abruptly pitched forwards in the air, flipping upside-down.

Alissa burst out laughing. "Okay, I see your point about the broomsticks."

"Glad you find my misfortune amusing." I attempted to step upright and somehow ended up standing at a horizontal angle. "Told you I have a hard enough time keeping upright with two feet on the ground."

"Are you going to buy those?" asked the sales assistant, a young witch with purple streaks in her black hair.

"Assuming I can get them off," I said. I took another step, and another, until I was the right away up again.

"We're almost out of the black ones," said the sales assistant. "Last order went out weeks ago. They're custom designed."

Hang on a moment. I looked down at my boot-clad feet. I'd seen someone else wearing an identical black pair recently. Apparently Wilfred Bloom shopped here. Since it was the only shoe shop, perhaps I shouldn't be surprised, but he hadn't levitated into the office. Probably for the best.

"Yes," said Alissa. "She is going to buy them."

"I shouldn't."

The assistant pointed her wand at the boots in my

hands and they jumped back into the shoebox. As she carried them to the desk, I whispered to Alissa, "I can't keep owing people. I'm still not certain I'll be keeping my job."

"Don't be ridiculous. I know you've had a trying week, but you won't get fired. Everyone likes you."

"One of my co-workers hates me and the other might be permanently stuck as a werewolf because I couldn't keep my nose out of an investigation that wasn't mine to begin with." And that wasn't even getting into the fact that I wasn't a witch. Veronica had been more or less shut in her office for the last two days when she wasn't driving us to finish our client lists in record time.

"Ah," she said. "I wouldn't worry. The few naysayers would change their minds pretty quickly if they found out you have a better way of getting the answers than Steve does."

"Don't the police have lie detectors?"

"There are potions, but they couldn't even narrow down the suspect list. You did that."

"Save the praise for when I actually figure out who did it," I said, blushing to the tips of my ears. "Also, I think he'll probably hate me more if I steal his glory. Anyway, you win. I'm getting the magical boots. I might have to give them another trial run before I try to fly over the lake."

"The lake," she said. "We can go and see that next. The falls, too."

Once the boots were wrapped up, we left the shop and continued down the cobbled street.

"If you meant it about the bubble wrap, I know a place," said Alissa.

"What, there's magical bubble wrap?" I asked.

"It re-inflates and repairs itself up to ten times."

I gave her a disbelieving look. "You're joking."

She smiled at my expression. "If I'd known you liked it so much, I'd have got you some."

I adjusted the bags I carried and continued to walk. "Who doesn't like bubble wrap? Especially the magical variety?"

"I know what to get you for your birthday, then."

My birthday wasn't until June. I hoped I'd get to stay here that long.

She led me to a stationery shop, which was packed with all manner of peculiarities ranging from pens with ink that changed colours to pencils jinxed to only write swear words.

"Oh. I'm in heaven," I announced, spotting a temptingly squishy stack of bubble wrap. The biggest packs would be enough to cover our entire flat.

"Told you," said Alissa.

"I can make it last a year." I pulled it off the shelf. "But I'm only getting the small one. And now I really need to stop spending my wages on junk."

"The boots might save your life someday," she said wisely. "All right—let's go and see the Fairy Falls and the lake."

She was in such a good mood, it was impossible not to pick up on her infectious energy, despite the muddy path leading to the lake.

"You'd think someone could magic away the mud," I said, grabbing her arm for the third time to keep from slipping over.

"It's great fertiliser. But those boots should help. Might stop you falling over in front Nathan, too."

I staggered upright. "Fainting and falling aren't the same thing."

"He's going to think you're weak at the knees for him."

"Pfft. I'd be weirded out if a guy kept falling on his face in front of me. And what if he guesses that it's because I haven't told him what I really am?" Would he mind? Considering how the werewolves had reacted last night, it was plain to see that he didn't get along with all the paranormals as well as Alissa had seemed to think.

"It's no big deal. There was a mix-up. It happens."

"Really?" I gave her a look. "And I suppose fairies who don't know what they are wander in here every day?"

"Maybe they do," she said. "Just not here."

"So inspiring."

"Hey, it's what makes you unique."

"Usually that's not a good thing." I trod carefully along the muddy path. "Sometimes it's nice to know *where* you fit."

"Don't you think you fit here? In spite of everything?"

"You know… I do. But I think I'm going to have to change into those boots as soon as I find somewhere dry to sit down."

I shoved the investigation firmly out of mind as we reached the lake. The water was pollution-free, and such a deep shade of blue that it looked like something out of the tropics. The surface was so clear up close that I could see every strand of the faintly glowing weeds, and faces hidden amongst the golden-tinted plants.

"Water imps. They bite."

I withdrew my hand quickly from where I'd caressed the cool water. "It's stunning."

"Isn't it?" She looked out across the lake's rippling surface. "There are boat races in summer," she said. "At the academy of magic. And they host various water sports."

"What are those?" I pointed to a group of human-shaped creatures with blue skin and seaweed-like hair. "Mermaids?"

"Nereids. Water fairies. They keep to themselves."

Fairy. Would they recognise me as one of them? They seemed more interested in frolicking and chasing their own tails, and I wasn't about to dive into the imp-infested water to join them.

"There are merpeople in there, too," she added, pointing

to a group of fish-tailed human-like creatures swimming with some witches in the shallows. "They wouldn't come ashore if they didn't like socialising with humans so much."

A group of broomsticks whirled overhead, and I stared up at them. "Isn't it a bit too cloudy for flying?"

"Not for them. They're the High Fliers Society. They're open for membership," she added.

"Yeah, no," I said, as the brooms flipped and glided through the air in motions that made me feel airsick even on the ground. "I don't mind flying, but that looks uncomfortable at best. Have you ever tried?"

"I used to be in the society, actually." She grinned a little. "Quit after a bad accident. Now I see enough of their injuries in the hospital to be put off ever joining them again."

"Makes sense." I watched the wheeling broomsticks, trying to imagine myself up there. As though wings might be there behind my shoulder blades. "Whereabouts are the falls?"

"This way." She beckoned me down a path alongside the lake. I kept one eye on the merpeople and the other on the sky, with the result that Alissa had to save me from falling into the water a few times. Eventually, we reached the foot of the rocky path leading to the falls.

The waterfall was even more impressive close up. Curtains of water cascaded down, throwing showers of glittering foam onto the bank.

I walked right up to the endlessly flowing water. "It's beautiful."

"Isn't it? They say it's made of fairy dust."

"In a literal sense?" I stepped as close as I could to the edge without slipping over into the water, reaching out a hand.

"I honestly have no idea."

Fairy dust.

I put my hand under the falls. Deliciously cool water, tinged with glitter, made my palm shimmer, but my hand looked the same when I pulled it out. Part of me wanted to dive in, but seeing those faces and hands in the water... maybe not. It was difficult to tell how deep the water was, but I'd never liked swimming much.

Glitter danced off the water, stirring a memory. When I'd escaped the collapsing mudslide, I was certain I'd seen an odd shimmer in the corners of my eyes. Had my fairy magic saved me?

We walked back to the town eventually. The sunset over the water was stunning, and I could hardly bear to drag my eyes away from the golden-tinted lake.

"Is the bookshop still open?" I asked Alissa. "I wanted to get a copy of that fairy book."

"We can detour that way," she said. "Oh hey—it's your friend."

Nathan walked towards us, his hands in his pockets. Even in casual wear, he had the manner of a man on a mission. I gave myself a mental shake for dwelling a little too long on the curl of dark hair falling into his eyes.

"Hey, Blair," he said. "Did you come to check out the falls?"

"Yeah, we're on our way back. It's so beautiful out here."

Alissa gave me a not-so-subtle nudge with her elbow. His gaze dropped to the carrier bags in my hands. "Bubble wrap?"

So much for keeping my dignity this time. Then again, anyone who didn't enable my bubble wrap obsession wasn't worth bothering with. "Yep. Don't judge me."

"I have a sister who loves that stuff."

Sister? It was the first time he'd mentioned family. Why couldn't he be the one I was interrogating? I guess you couldn't have it all.

"What're you here for?" I asked.

"I'm here to keep an eye on the High Fliers," he said. "Just in case any of them fall into the lake and start a fight with the nereids."

"Is that likely?" I asked.

"Yes, unfortunately," said Alissa. "Luckily I'm not working tonight."

"See you around, Blair," he added. Alissa nudged me again. I pretended not to notice until he was out of sight.

"Is he ever not on duty?" I said to her.

"Sure, when he's taking you for dates in coffee shops."

"Oi. Enough match-making. I told you I'm not ready for a relationship, here or otherwise. I need to get a handle on life, first."

"You have more of a handle on it than they do." She pointed to the sky, where the broomstick-riding witches and wizards appeared to have created a pile-up in mid-air.

"Oops," I said. "Can't they use a spell on the broomsticks to stop people falling off them?"

"Technically, but it's not fool-proof, and the High Fliers insist it'd ruin the fun. Anyway, stop diverting. You like him. Didn't fall over this time, either."

"No, but I didn't fall the first time. I was sitting on the floor of my own free will." She had a point. I was soaking wet from the falls, but no mud or floors were involved this time. An improvement.

As we reached the bookshop, a pitiful meowing noise came from the doorstep. I glanced down and spotted a black cat with a white paw. One of its eyes was grey, the other was a startling blue. "The bookshop's cat?"

"No idea. Looks like it's closed, though—we can come back tomorrow. I think that cat wants to come with us."

Sure enough, the cat got to its feet and padded after us.

"You already have a cat," I pointed out.

"Maybe he's your familiar."

"I'm not supposed to have a familiar," I said. "I'm not a witch."

"Miaow." The cat was right behind me.

"Seriously," I said. "I'm not in a position to adopt anything."

The cat kept following. I'd never even kept a plant alive, let alone an animal. But he looked so bedraggled. Maybe there was an animal shelter or somewhere to take him to.

"See?" she said. "He likes you."

"He thinks I have food. I can't keep a pet."

"Says who? We're allowed all the animals we want. The landlord doesn't care as long as they don't mess up the garden."

"I'm not good with animals. When I was at school, I was entrusted with looking after the class's pet snails."

"Pet *snails?*" She wrinkled her nose.

"There was no budget for a hamster. Anyway, the snails escaped and were never seen again." I'd spent hours running around in the rain looking for substitutes. The teacher never noticed, luckily, so I got away with that one.

"Cats are intelligent and well-behaved."

"Miaow," said the cat, from behind us, as though agreeing with her point.

"Do they understand English?"

"Familiars do. Hmm."

"I'm not a witch," I said ineffectually. We'd reached the road to the house by that point. "Is there an animal shelter somewhere here?"

"Yes, there is, but that cat is coming in whether you like it or not. Trust me, witch cats are not to be argued with."

"I think the same goes for all cats in general, but I'm not ready for a pet." I walked into the hall behind her. "Anyway, what if the coven finds out?"

"You won't be punished for adopting a stray. But I do think you need to tell Madame Grey you've used magic."

Easier said than done. "How can I explain the levitation without mentioning the mudslide incident?"

"Say you fell at the falls… oh. The lies."

"Exactly." I groaned. "This is a pain. I wouldn't say I lie *all* the time, but who doesn't?"

The cat raised a paw. "Miaow."

"Can you translate that?" I asked.

"No, I don't speak cat."

The cat stalked decisively ahead of us into the flat the instant Alissa opened the door, and sat on the sofa.

"I think *I* just got adopted," I said. "You have spare cat food, right? I'd have bought some if I knew I was going to become a pet owner."

"Sure."

Roald padded up to the sofa, sniffing at the newcomer. The cat swatted at Roald, who retaliated with a yowl and swipe.

"Feline wars," I said. "Told you this was a bad idea."

"I think it's a great idea, actually. He needs to learn boundaries."

"Now I need to pick up a *Magical Cats for Dummies* guide, too." I walked to the kitchen and opened the cupboard where Alissa kept the cat food. The little cat appeared at my side so fast, it might well have teleported. "There," I said, tipping cat food into a bowl. "Don't look at me like that, it's not like I planned to get a familiar. You're going to have to stop fighting with Roald if you want to stay."

I put the bowl down and moved the bags containing my new boots and the bubble wrap to my bedroom. "I know how I can give the boots for a spin. I need to test the boundaries of this weird lying curse thing, but somewhere it won't be a hazard if I fall over."

ELLE ADAMS

"Good idea," Alissa said. "You might want to wait until you've gained some control over those boots, though."

"Maybe you're right. Okay, I'll do it this way." After checking the cat wasn't behind me, I stood in front of the sofa and said, "I'm a witch."

No reaction.

"I'm a werewolf."

I held my breath, but I didn't fall back like I had in the shop. There was a loud popping noise from the bedroom. The cat had disappeared, leaving his bowl empty.

"Crap." I ran into the bedroom. The cat sat surrounded by dismembered bubble wrap, wearing a piteous expression.

"I already fed you."

"Miaow."

"That was to get my attention? Alissa, isn't that bubble wrap meant to repair itself?"

Muffled laughter came from behind me. "It is. But not from that state."

I narrowed my eyes at the small feline. "You're not a stray, are you?"

"Miaow."

I picked up the sheet of shredded bubble wrap. "Miaow yourself. Go and kill some mice or something. There have to be some around here, right?"

I deposited the wrecked bubble wrap in the bin. The cat followed, padding confidently after me.

"We're testing my fairy powers," I told him. "See, I'm a fairy. Not a witch. Alissa already has a familiar. And if you're not careful, I'll end up falling on you."

"Miaow."

"Are you sure you're trying the right lies?" said Alissa.

"Who even knows." I rolled my eyes. "My whole life has been one little white lie after another. Lucky this didn't happen in my last customer service job. I'd have passed out

148

behind the counter every time someone demanded to speak to the manager… actually, that wouldn't have been so bad."

"Dealing with normals sounds awful." She sat in the armchair, Roald curled on her lap.

"Isn't it like that here? Don't you get angry wizard patients being obnoxious?"

"Yes, but we have earplug charms." She grinned.

"You're making me more and more keen to stay here forever. Even if they don't keep me at Eldritch & Co. I never want to have to listen to someone tell me to make them a cappuccino and then scream at me for not making a latte instead again."

"One spell would take care of that problem."

So it would. "Can't I use magic at all outside of the town?"

"No," she said. "I mean, theoretically you can, now your powers have actually awakened, but there are rules. As I'm sure Madame Grey has drilled into you by now."

"Unfortunately, yes." I rearranged the cushions on the sofa to form a soft landing. "Maybe the effect depends on the strength of the lie. If I tell a huge one, then… let's hope I fall in the right direction."

"I'll catch you."

"I'm a tadpole."

Nothing happened.

"Oh, come on," I said. "I'm seventy-five years old and I like hiking and bright pink socks."

Nothing.

Alissa pursed her lips. "What exactly kicked this off in the first place?"

My face flamed. "Nathan asked if I was interested in fairies because he caught me red-handed holding a book. I panicked and said I wasn't. Definitely not the biggest lie I've ever told. I once pretended to be fluent in Spanish in a job interview. That was an adventure."

She snorted. "Maybe it's situational. I don't know enough about fairy magic to be sure. Or maybe because you found him attractive and panicked."

"I panicked because I thought he might have arrested or killed fairies in the past. *Has* he?"

"I don't know. Maybe ask?"

"And get caught in a lie when he asks why I want to know?"

"Good point." She reached to pet Roald, who'd tensed up when the new cat walked past him. "I don't think it's lying that's the problem."

My own cat was watching me wearing an expression I could only describe as *'what is that crazy woman doing?'*

"It's okay for some people," I told it. "You're a cat. You can do whatever you like and nobody will judge you for it. You aren't failing at being a fairy and a witch at the same time."

The cat yawned and started washing itself.

"You aren't failing at anything," said Alissa. "If anything, you're coping admirably well. Also, familiar or not, it's generally not a good idea to ask for life advice from a cat."

"I suppose I should name it," I said dubiously. "It's a he, right?"

"Yes, he is."

"Okay... how do you like the name Paws?"

The cat shook his whiskers, like he thought I was dense.

"Too obvious? Okay... how about Sky?"

He licked its paw, which I assumed meant approval, and bounded onto the arm of Alissa's chair. Roald hissed at him.

"You haven't won this," I said. "Fairies don't have familiars. You're staying here on the condition that you don't bully any other animals, got it?"

"Miaow." He took another swipe at Roald. Alissa leapt from her seat as Feline Wars Part 2 erupted.

Oh boy. This is going to be an adventure.

14

I went into work on Monday in a much better mood, despite the spectre of Mr Bayer's unsolved murder and Callie's situation hanging over me. Partly it was due to my new levitating boots, which I'd eventually got the hang of after a series of hair-raising mishaps yesterday. Or maybe it was because I'd been too preoccupied chasing my new cat to dwell on the investigation.

With our leads gone, the only option was to sneakily call the three rejected people again and hope they wouldn't bite my head off this time. And also hope that I didn't get found out by a certain police officer. Or anyone else, for that matter. Two of the interviewees were out of work, which *did* give me a good enough excuse to speak with them and find out if they were interested in working with Eldritch & Co again.

I skimmed through today's client list to find a likely position that would fit one of the candidates. Eventually, I came across one. Vaughn would fit the bill—without having to pretend to be magically talented or disclose his werewolf nature.

I dialled the number.

"Yes?" the werewolf rasped tersely. "What do you want this time?"

"I found the perfect placement for you," I told him. "But before I arrange an interview for you, I'm going to need you to answer a few questions first. Honestly."

"Yes?" he said warily.

"Are you a werewolf?"

There came the immediate sound of a dial tone. I waited a few seconds, then called him back.

"I'm not—"

"If you weren't, you wouldn't have hung up on me," I told him. "The day after your fight with Callie, she turned full wolf and hasn't recovered. Know anything?"

"No. Why would I?"

"She knew what you were," I said. "It's nothing to be ashamed of, but the legal implications of hiding your status from the pack would create a situation for my colleagues and myself which I'd frankly prefer not to deal with. It doesn't matter to this client, either way."

"If this isn't confidential," he rasped, "I'll... I'll."

"That sounds like a threat. Mr Llewellyn—"

"Okay, okay, I'm a werewolf," he said. "I don't want anything to do with the pack. Any of them."

I thought of the band at the New Moon. I'd want to avoid that, too.

"What about shifting at the full moon? You do that, right? Isn't that... dangerous?" I didn't know every detail of how the pack worked, but I *did* know that safety was their number one priority.

"I have someone who locks my room when I transform so I don't escape. Why? Has someone been attacked by a wolf?"

"No, my colleague's been permanently turned *into* a wolf.

At least, none of us can turn her back. We're pretty sure it's a spell. Has it ever happened before?"

"I've been outside the werewolf community for years. I don't know. You mean Callie, right? They're saying Mr Bayer's murderer did it."

"Yes," I said. "That's what we think, anyway, but since none of us has been able to take the spell off, naturally we had to think of the last time a werewolf came into our office. Callie recognised you and you stormed off."

"I didn't attack her," he said defensively. "You know I don't have any magic. If I'd started a fight with her, you'd have found both of us brawling until one of us passed out."

His words carried a ring of truth. "Assuming I believe you, we still need to find who did it."

"The killer? Why not finish her off?"

"Haven't a clue." He had a point, though. But inept or not, the killer had tried to get me eaten alive by killer plants. Not an act of a person who'd let the innocent office assistant get away alive—right? "It's not like any of us has a wolf's senses. We still don't know if the spell was cast from inside the office."

"If it was, I'd be able to sniff it out," he said. "Tell you what —can I come and talk to you in person again?"

"You can sniff out spells that are several days old?"

"Yes, I can."

"Okay, I'll clear a space on my schedule at noon."

Sorted. I could deal with today's paperwork before then— and maybe get to the bottom of the case. He wasn't a bad guy after all, for a temperamental werewolf.

I returned to my inbox, noticing Blythe glance at me over the desk. She'd probably been reading my thoughts, so it wasn't like I could pretend to have been on script, but I hardly cared. *He can sniff out the villain.* Callie could, too, but she wasn't able to communicate with us despite our best efforts. I pretended not to notice when Blythe got to her feet and walked over to my desk.

"Hey, fairy," Blythe hissed in my ear.

I turned slowly towards her. "Blythe. What can I do for you this fine morning?"

"You," she said, "need to stop."

"You'll have to be a little more specific than that. If you're reading my thoughts, then it's not my problem if you don't like what you hear."

"I can't believe you have the nerve to invite *another* murder suspect into the office."

"Same one as last time, actually." I gave her a smile. "I'd have thought you'd want to clear up who attacked Callie."

"Not by threatening all our safety," she said.

"Relax, we have a security werewolf."

She snorted. "Yes, we do. Better than the other security we had. He was far too easily distracted." Her words were knowing. She'd definitely picked up on my wayward thoughts about Nathan at one point or another.

"There you have it. Go back to work."

"I could report you," she said.

"You could. But the boss didn't bat an eyelid the last time I invited him here."

"And have you told her the truth yet?" she said. "You're no witch. This office is for witches. *Four* witches."

"Wouldn't it be even worse luck not to *have* a fourth member?" I pointed out. I didn't believe in superstitions, and if it'd been any real issue, the others would have brought it up. I pointedly picked up the phone. "If you don't mind, I have a call to make."

She huffed and stalked away, while Bethan shot me a sideways look. "I wouldn't provoke her."

"She's doing a spectacular job of provoking *me*. Besides, I think I'm close to solving this." I'd met too many petty people like her in the normal world to be put off by her constant grumbling.

"I'm not disputing that, but there's a risk. If he's guilty—"

"It's not illegal to hide your paranormal type, is it?" I said. "We still have no evidence he committed a crime. But he might be able to sniff out who did it." And I wasn't about to toss an innocent man into jail. I'd heard the paranormal prison wasn't a pleasant place, and Steve the Gargoyle was unlikely to give anyone the benefit of the doubt.

"Do you really want to push your luck?" she said.

"No, but the sooner we deal with this case, the better for everyone." I heard the creak of the front door opening from the reception. "He's not supposed to be here until noon."

"Ah." Bethan leapt to her feet. "The boss—"

"Incoming," Lizzie warned, and the printer made a growling noise which might have been a warning, too.

Veronica's sharp voice carried through the slightly open office door. "What are you doing here?"

I looked at Blythe in disbelief. She'd told the boss. I shot her a glare. *Seriously?* How had she even known he'd arrive early? I left my files in disarray and hurried out of the office. That's what I got for making reckless decisions.

Veronica stood beside the desk, her wand in her hand, while two huge werewolves filled the rest of the area. Positioned nose to nose, they growled at one another.

"There seems to be an unregistered werewolf in here," Veronica said.

"Really?" I said weakly. He was huge. Twice Callie's size, with a long face and *teeth.* Oh no. I hadn't even had the presence of mind to grab any silver.

"Callie!" said the boss. "Lie down."

She growled in answer.

"Did he do it?" I mouthed at Callie, indicating the other werewolf.

ELLE ADAMS

She let out a whine and shook her head a little before lowering her paws obediently. I looked at the boss in surprise.

"He's tame. Just had a shock, didn't you?" Veronica sounded like a pet owner comforting her dog after a thunderstorm.

Everyone else wore expressions of varying degrees of confusion, except Blythe. Steam might as well have been coming out of her ears. "There is a werewolf in here."

"Yes, there is," said Veronica. "She's worked here longer than you have."

I nearly laughed that time. The second werewolf let out a whine, then turned human again.

"Vaughn Llewellyn, is it?" said Veronica. "I've had my eye on your case for a while."

He drooped his head, his shaggy hair falling into his eyes. "How do you know who I am?"

"You've used our services multiple times," Veronica observed. "I assumed you had good reason to hide your real identity?"

I wheeled to face her. "You knew?" *Then he can't be the killer.* My boss might be a little eccentric, but she wouldn't let a murderer walk in here. Not with her alleged paranoia about security.

"I had my suspicions. Are you ready to turn yourself into the pack now?"

He made a whining noise not unlike his wolf form. "Chief Donovan? Please, no."

I snorted. I couldn't help it. Even Callie looked sympathetic, though it was difficult to read facial expressions on a wolf.

"All right," he muttered. "I'll tell them. Just as long as they don't make me play the guitar."

"I think a cat could do a better job than their current

bassist," I said.

All eyes turned to me. Oops.

"She's right," said Veronica.

I was starting to worry Blythe's head might actually explode. "You *knew* he was an unregistered werewolf?" she asked, through teeth so tightly clenched, her voice dimmed to a low whine not unlike said werewolf.

"At this point, the whole office does," said Veronica mildly. "You didn't have a problem bringing up the subject at the coven meeting this weekend, Blythe. Blair, dearest, I'd like a word with you later."

My heart sank. Despite her lack of concern, it *was* technically my fault he'd come into the office in the first place, but it looked less and less like he was actually responsible for the attack on Callie, let alone the murder. Unless his guilty conscience was an act, but surely the boss would have seen through it if it was. "Okay. Do you need someone to take him to the pack?"

I expected her to ask Nathan, not that he was around to witness the latest debacle. Instead, she said, "Go with him, Blair. Take him to register with the pack. It'll be good experience for you."

Oh no. That meant another encounter with Callie's father. The boss might be on my side for now, but what did she want to talk to me about? At least she seemed to think Blythe was as big an idiot as I did.

The werewolf looked even more downcast than I felt as we left the office.

"I got you into trouble, didn't I?" he said.

"I got *myself* into trouble," I said. "And you. What will they do to you when they find out?"

"Probably assign me to sound engineer duty."

I winced. "Ow. Do you really have to be involved with the band at all?"

"No, but the beta is in charge of dealing out punishments, and he finds it amusing."

I found it incredibly hard to believe Alissa had lasted long in a relationship with him. "You seem to know a lot about the pack, considering you've never been a member."

"So do you. How'd you know what I was? You knew before she did."

"Callie told me."

I had barely a second's warning before the ground surged towards my face. I managed to throw my hands out to break my fall and turned my boots on, but not before the impact tore through my knees and elbows. *Ouch.* So much for the levitating boots solving all my problems.

"Whoa." He reached out a hand uncertainly. "Are you okay?"

"Yes. I just felt light-headed." I was glad Nathan wasn't here to witness it this time, but I'd bet Blythe was watching from the window. "Come on. I need to get you to the pack. How do you register, exactly? Go to the leader?"

"Yes, but first I need to talk to Madame Grey. She's the one who keeps the list of each paranormal in town."

"A *list?* Why, to stop more normals wandering in?" Or to stop people from hiding their identities like he did? I didn't dislike the leader of the witches, but the idea didn't sit right with me. Nor did how easily he'd volunteered to give himself up.

"It's tradition. There are so few of us left."

"What, the werewolf population is dying out or something? How'd you end up hiding your identity, anyway?"

He shrugged. "Have you tried getting work as a werewolf? We lose all reason during the full moon. A lot of employers see it as a safety hazard. Since I was born outside of town and adopted by witches, I saw no reason to tell anyone."

Adopted. "Is that common? I mean, being adopted by another paranormal group?" *As opposed to humans?*

"No," he said. "Especially with werewolves. The pack is very family-oriented and I'd never feel like I belonged there."

A knot formed in my chest. He wasn't a bad guy. Or maybe it was the similarities between our own situations that made me want to trust him.

"So… your applications. You must have known you'd lose out against someone who had the proper qualifications?"

He hesitated before answering, "I guess. I didn't know Mr Bayer was looking for an actual assistant and not just someone to clean up after him until I showed up for the interview."

Lie. I almost stopped walking. Which part was a lie? That was one serious downside of my ability. "Really?" I asked, carefully. "So you must have spoken to the previous assistant…"

He nodded. My ability didn't kick in, but maybe it only responded to words, not gestures.

"Well?" I prompted. "What happened in the interview? Was there a reason you chose him? Surely he'd have guessed you weren't a wizard even if you didn't have to actually use magic."

"Yeah, he's clever," said Vaughn. "Okay. I admit it. I wanted to see his new spell."

"New spell?" I echoed.

He dropped his gaze. "He didn't talk about it, but some rumours got out that he was building a spell that blocks certain types of magic. His last assistant accidentally let it slip, and word made it back to me. I guess the prototype was lost after he died, but it was meant to be a shield spell."

"From mind-reading?" I recalled hearing the same rumour. "Ah. Of course—that'd give you away."

And it had. Blythe would have known what he was

without having to read *my* mind, yet I'd bet she wouldn't have volunteered that information. She probably knew everyone's secrets in town, if she only needed to be in the same room as them to read their minds.

A suspicion took root inside me. "So did you see the spell?"

"Of course I didn't," he said. "I failed the interview."

And now the spell has gone. He didn't have it—surely Blythe would have told someone if he did, considering its potential dangers. I did *not* want to have a conversation with her after the downright murderous look she'd given me, but I'd know if she was lying.

Suddenly, I wished I hadn't left the office at all. And not just because my knees and elbows were seriously starting to smart from where I'd fallen earlier.

We reached the coven's meeting place. I relaxed a little when he walked ahead of me through the wide oak doors and Madame Grey was in the entrance hall, in conversation with a teenage witch. He wouldn't try anything in front of her. But how to extricate myself and run back to the office? Pity I *couldn't* teleport.

Perhaps Blythe was right after all. My attempting to defuse any situation somehow caused it to morph into a Lovecraftian Monster of a problem. Maybe Eldritch & Co had been aptly named.

"Yes?" she asked, spotting me. "Is there a problem?"

"I have someone here who'd like to register as a member of the local werewolf pack." I indicated Vaughn.

The teenage girl squinted at him. "A new wolf? He looks a little old for a first-time shifter."

He shuffled his feet. "Yeah, I missed the first cut-off point."

More like secretly registered as a wizard instead. It seemed awfully easy to register as something you weren't.

You'd think they'd be more careful, given the number of tests witches and wizards apparently had to do. Surely someone else would have run a search on his degree at the very least. Employers in the human world did. And for a position like an assistant spellmaker, you'd think they'd want to check if their candidates were actually qualified beforehand. Then again, that was Dritch & Co's job...

My phone buzzed with a message, startling me—more because it hadn't happened since I'd been here than anything else. The message was from Callie, and contained a jumble of letters that made no sense. Like a wolf paw hitting a phone.

"I have to get back to work." I assumed that's what Callie had tried to type—but why did I feel like I'd missed something vital? "Can you take it from here?"

I didn't wait for her response. I left the building and broke into a jog. What if Callie was in trouble again? She'd known *something*, and was unable to tell anyone who her attacker was. And Vaughn's story had far more holes than it should have.

Nathan was outside the office, and his gaze immediately went to my muddy feet. "Blair? What happened to you?"

"I was helping the werewolves. Is Callie okay?"

"Yes. Why?"

I breathed out. "She sent me a text message that was mostly gibberish. I thought she might have been attacked again."

"Werewolves?" he asked, sounding wary. "What were you doing with them?"

"One of our clients wanted to register with the pack. I need to talk to—"

He frowned. "Wait, you invited the murder suspect back again? Did he do that to you?"

I followed his gaze, belatedly remembering my shredded knees. "That was an accident. None of the wolves attacked

161

me, don't worry. I left him with Madame Grey." I glimpsed Blythe through the window. "Did Blythe do anything while I was gone?"

"Do anything?" he echoed. "Like what?"

"She's had it in for me since the moment I stepped into the office. You'd think I put dead pigeons in the water tank or something. Know why?"

"No, but I did see her speaking to Veronica."

My mouth went dry. "Right. I should go… report in."

His hand briefly touched my arm. "Relax. I'm not blaming you. If anything, you're handling the situation like a pro. But even the witches have trouble getting the werewolves under control."

"And if they fail, they send you after them?"

He blinked. "If I'm needed, yes."

"Are you slacking off out there?" Blythe called through the window.

"No," I called back. "Don't get all agitated. I'm on my way back in."

Blythe laughed. "First I've heard. Don't feel too sorry for her, Nathan. If you want the real truth, ask her why she can't lie."

He turned slowly to me, confusion furrowing his brow. "What was that about?"

"Noth—" Oh no. "She has it in for me. Like I said."

"Truth," he said. "You can tell if people are lying. Is that your gift? Is that why you took over the investigation?"

"It is, but that's not the only reason."

"So why wouldn't *you* be able to lie?"

I shrugged one shoulder. "I'm still trying to figure out my magic."

"All right. It's none of my business. I should get back to work."

I couldn't tell from his tone if he was annoyed with me.

No—more like disappointed. I had nobody to blame but myself for not coming up with a decent cover story, much less accidentally antagonising the werewolves and probably making his life more difficult as well. And now Blythe had all but told him I was one of the misbehaving paranormals he'd probably come here to get away from.

I walked back into the building, past Callie, who let out a whining noise.

"I know the feeling," I said to her. "Don't worry. I'm going to try to fix this."

At least the boss was still in her office, but the idea of facing Blythe was about as appealing as joining the High Fliers.

"Yeah, I know I look like hell warmed over," I said to a startled-looking Bethan. "I don't suppose you have a first-aid spell?"

"Did the wolf do that?"

"Nope, I tripped. Let's never speak of it again." I heard Blythe's laughter, but tuned it out. "I'm going to clean up."

I went into the toilets to compose myself. My reflection in the mirror above the sinks was a disaster. My hair was a tangled windswept mess, and there was mud all down my legs and on my shoes. Blythe's smirk was the last straw. I made a mental note to look up how to hex someone you disliked and got about cleaning myself up.

Hex someone you dislike...

The words floated around my head and then halted in the forefront of my mind, along with the image of an open window.

Wait a moment.

I made my way back to my desk, where Bethan waited.

"I can fix your clothes." She waved her wand, and my shredded knees repaired themselves.

"Thank you." I returned to my seat. "Why did Callie text

me, do you know?"

"She did? Maybe she put her paw on the phone by accident."

I glanced up at Blythe, thinking carefully about anything except—hang on. The werewolf's notes lay on the desk where I hadn't put them away, and there was a detail I hadn't noticed before.

He *had* passed the interview. Was that what he'd lied to me about?

"Something up?" asked Bethan.

"Is it possible for someone to use magic without using their own wand? Or to fake it?"

Bethan frowned. "Why?"

"Werewolf dude cheated on his entry exams," I said. "He's not a wizard but he got the qualifications somehow. Wouldn't Mr Bayer have had him do a practical test?"

I *knew* I'd overlooked something.

She pursed her lips. "Yes. He'll have had to prove he could cast certain spells."

"So did he borrow someone's wand, or...?"

"You can't cast spells using someone else's wand," she said. "Maybe someone else did it... but they'd have to be in the room. Or outside, I guess... if there was a window open."

"Because you can't cast spells through solid objects," I said, recalling Rita's lesson. "But surely Mr Bayer would have noticed someone else in the room.

Unless the window was open.

Someone had helped him cheat. Someone with access to powerful magic. If it'd been one of the other candidates, they'd have had to be close by... and nobody aside from them had had access to the testing room. Maybe Mr Bayer had found out about the cheating and they'd killed him to cover it up.

I think we have a motive.

15

"I left him with Madame Grey," I said to Bethan. "He won't try anything with her, I wouldn't think. He seemed so… genuine."

I lifted Vaughn's file aside. I'd been so sure. I should have just *asked* if he'd killed Mr Bayer, but he had an accomplice.

Maybe one who'd committed the murder to help him cover his tracks.

"It's not just the werewolf thing," Bethan said, tapping her computer keyboard. "He's faked his way through a dozen other job trials, at least. He's been paying someone to cover for him. Someone with magical abilities."

"I thought so," I said. "But—who?"

The printer spat a wad of paper at me. Through sheer luck, I actually caught it this time. According to the records, Vaughn had applied for two more positions in Fairy Falls and had passed the practical element of each interview with flying colours. His name appeared on multiple lists, but I could only find two jobs which had required a specific practical test which would have required him to use a wand.

"Bethan," I said, "is it possible for you to find the list of the other candidates who applied for these two positions?" I held up the page to indicate the two highlighted examples. "There was a practical test involved both times."

"On it." Her hands skimmed the keyboard faster than I'd have thought any human could move. "It depends on the employer, but most wizards are wise to trickery. He must have worked with a highly adept spellcaster... but wow. They must have been *really* good."

"Like Wilfred Bloom?" He was the most accomplished spellcaster of the remaining two interviewees, and the most likely not to care about the consequences of using magic on behalf of someone else.

Bethan paused in her typing. "Yes. He applied for the last job, too." She turned to me. "Want to call him in again?"

I shook my head. "It's too obvious. I'm missing something. Besides, the other employers are still alive and kicking."

"Because they didn't catch him?"

"No, they didn't. But he's... are you absolutely certain it's not possible for someone to cast spells on behalf of someone else?"

"It might be, but he *has* a wand. He must have, otherwise they wouldn't have let him into the interview."

"I didn't even consider that angle. Did he definitely have a real wand?"

"Apparently." Bethan cast her gaze around and it landed on Lizzie. "Hey, Lizzie. How would one go about acquiring a black-market wand?"

Lizzie glanced up. "You couldn't pay me to speak to the wand-maker again, but he's the only person in the town who has the authority to sell a wand to someone."

"That's it," said Bethan. "The wand-maker will know."

"The one everyone hates?" I'd heard from multiple sources that the man was a notorious grump. But if anyone might be able to guess what'd gone down in the interview, he would. And she raised a good point—*how* had Vaughn acquired a wand? Maybe from his witch family, but the vast number of witchcraft laws would surely have got in the way at some point.

"Him," said Bethan. "Better make it quick. The boss is in a mood."

My heart sank. Veronica wanted to speak to me after work. Doubtlessly, she'd either had enough of my habit of causing chaos, or she knew I wasn't a witch. Neither of those things would help me in any way with resolving this crime, and I *was* close. I knew it. The possible culprit was already in Madame Grey's hands, and yet…

I dialled the wand-maker's number. A male voice answered. My senses told me he was a wizard. No surprises there.

"Hello, it's Blair from Eldritch & Co."

"What do you want?" he growled.

"I was wondering… do you often sell wands to non-wizards? Or wizards?"

"Are you making fun of me? Wands are for wizards only."

"Let me explain," I hastened to add. "I'm new in town, and there's been an incident involving someone cheating at an interview in which they may have either stolen someone else's wand or used some kind of substitute. I wanted to know if it was possible."

He growled. "Certainly *not*. If the wand doesn't choose them, then it won't work. No exceptions. We only sell to witches or wizards."

"The person I'm talking about was an unqualified wizard. Unless… is it possible to cast spells on behalf of someone else?"

"Wait, aren't you the unqualified detective who's causing the police no end of hassle?"

ELLE ADAMS

Oh great. He would be friends with Steve the ever-grumpy gargoyle. I pushed on, trying to ignore the instinct that this was a monumentally terrible idea. "Then... have you ever sold a wand to Mr Vaughn Llewellyn?"

"Customer information is confidential."

Of course it was. I needed to find out more about what'd gone down in the interview in order to work out if he'd cast the spells himself or if it'd been possible for someone else to interfere. You couldn't cast spells through solid objects... so the window must have been open.

It was on the top floor. That'd make it tricky to aim. Unless the accomplice had levitated—

Levitate. Those boots were almost out of stock... and I'd seen Wilfred wearing them when he came into the office.

There were a million ways of doing a levitation charm. But not if you were casting spells on someone else's behalf through the open window of an interview room at the same time. You could only cast one spell at once.

I hung up. "Wow."

Bethan said, "Yes, he really is that rude to everyone. Sometimes I'm surprised new witches and wizards acquire wands at all."

"Well, he got all insulted that I implied he was selling wands under the table," I said. "But I don't think that's what happened."

Bethan frowned. "No. Someone else must have been help-ing. I'd almost say it's impossible to cast spells in such a way as to make it look like someone else did it... if the killer is capable of that, they're capable of worse. This is way beyond my level."

Tell me about it. But I thought I knew the story. At the interview, Vaughn had paid Wilfred to help him fake being a competent spellcaster. He'd done so by casting the spells from outside the room in order to make it look like Vaughn

168

had done it. And then… and then I guessed one of the two of them had killed Mr Bayer, perhaps because he'd found out about the cheating. With those boots, Wilfred could also have levitated into the garden and found the poison that way. And Vaughn had handed himself in…

Because the pack would defend him. They protected their own. Like a fool, I'd let him hand himself over to the people most likely to bare their fangs in defence of him—and who already hated me.

I couldn't have screwed this up more thoroughly if I tried.

Bethan squinted at me. "Are you okay, Blair? You look a little pale."

"I …" I trailed off. With the pack behind him, things could get nasty. Unless Madame Grey had figured out his game. But nothing about my conclusions accounted for Callie's indifference when he showed up. He hadn't put the spell on her to make the pack turn on me. I'd done that on my own.

I took in a breath. "I'm going to call Madame Grey. Then I'll talk to the boss."

———

I left the boss's office to find Blythe standing outside. "What are you doing?" she asked.

"You'll be pleased to know we caught the perpetrator," I told her. "So we're handing this over to the police."

Her brows shot up. "What?"

"Yes. He's coming back here first, so he can reverse the spell on Callie." I watched her face carefully for any changes in expression.

I'd heard a lot of people lie over the last week. Some were more obvious than others. My magic told the truth, including the unspoken truth. When I knew what to look for, that is. And Blythe looked like she was trying to suck on a lemon.

"Go on," I said. "What is it? Something wrong with my plan? You want Callie back in her human form, or…"

"You can stop gloating," she growled.

"Are you going to tell the boss you did it?" I asked. "Because it's not looking good for you, either. If you've been listening to my thoughts, not to mention the candidates', you'll already know who the killer is. Yet you chose not to tell anyone and attacked your own colleague instead."

"Because you're not the bloody police," she said. "It was going to get you both killed. And for the record, no, I didn't pick up anything from the suspects' thoughts, but they're *all* angry with you. Leaving it to the police is the best move."

"That's exactly the plan," I said. "Thanks for leading me down a false trail that nearly got me killed."

"If you didn't run into trouble at every turn, none of this would have happened."

"Mr Bayer died before I was even here," I countered. "I'm starting to think *you're* the bad luck charm in the office. Anyway, as I said, the police are taking over. So you can go back to worrying that I'm killing your vibe or whatever it is."

I walked past her to the lobby. Callie lay beside the desk, her head resting on her paws. When she saw Blythe, she let out a low growl.

"Go on," I said to her. "Reverse the spell. I think Callie's spent long enough stuck in that form."

Blythe scowled. Then with a flick of her wand, Callie jumped backwards. The desk went flying, somewhat ruining my triumph in a shower of papers and stationary. But a second later, in place of the wolf was a dishevelled Callie.

Lizzie and Bethan ran from the office into the lobby. "Callie!"

She shook her head, looking dazed. "I've been wearing the same clothes for days."

"You've been wearing fur for days," said Lizzie. "Where's the caster?"

I gave Blythe a pointed look. "Right here. Meanwhile, Veronica is in contact with the police about the murderer, who is also in custody. Unless you want to confess to that, too?"

"You don't have to act so smug," said Blythe. "No, I'm not a murderer. I didn't kill anyone, or order anyone else to do it, so you can stop looking at me like you have a clue what I'm thinking."

Callie shook her head again. "I don't remember much."

"I'll let Blythe explain."

One perpetrator down. One to go. But despite my near-certainty about how the events of the interview had played out, Blythe was innocent of murder. *I didn't kill anyone... or order anyone else to do it.* Her jaw was set stubbornly, determined to make life difficult even as she knew she'd lost.

I'd left the interview files on the desk. Running into the office, I picked them up one-handed. Wilfred had helped Vaughn cheat—no disputing it—but the only way to know if any other foul play had occurred was to talk to the wizard himself again.

I picked up the phone and called Wilfred Bloom. I expected a dial tone, but he picked up. "Hello?"

"Hey. It's Blair," I said quickly. "Blair Wilkes, from Dritch & Co."

"Oh, hi," he said brightly. "What's up?"

Nope, the coven definitely hadn't called him yet. "Er, you might get a phone call from Madame Grey, or the police. Any second now, actually. It's about, er, Vaughn Lewellyn."

There was a long pause. "Shoot," he muttered.

"Sorry." I was fairly sure that someone who'd committed

murder would have said a stronger word than 'shoot' when cornered. But... "Why?"

"Mother cut off my allowance. For failing too many interviews."

Ah. "So he paid you to cheat?"

"It didn't do any harm," he said defensively.

"It might have," I said. "You know Mr Bayer died immediately afterwards, right? Did he catch you?"

"No, I left after the interview. I did tell you that, right?"

"Yes. You also told me Vaughn threw a temper tantrum." Now I knew he'd helped the werewolf, drawing attention to him did seem kind of odd. Vaughn had pretended never to have met the wizard in his life when I'd interviewed him, but that was to be expected. Wilfred was supposed to be the smarter of the two, based on his memory powers at least, but he sure didn't act like it.

"I guess I did," he said, sounding puzzled. "Huh. Dunno why I did that."

Honestly. "What did you do after the interview, then?"

"Went home and put my feet up," he said immediately.

Lie.

"Are you sure about that?"

"Yes."

Truth.

What? Was my lie-sensing power broken?

"You're sure but you didn't?"

"What the bloody hell does that mean?" He sounded irritated now. "Am I getting arrested or what? If I need to pay a fine, I'll ask my mother—"

"What did you do after the interview?"

"Went home. Put my feet up."

Lie. Not broken, then. "Are you sure you didn't see Mr Bayer before you left?"

"Why do you keep asking the same questions?" His face

showed confusion in my mind's eye. "I didn't see him. He was gonna interview the last candidate, Simeon whatsit, so I left."

Lie... true.

Okay, this was too much. If my lie-sensing ability couldn't be trusted, I'd have to leave it to Madame Grey.

"Sorry," I said to him. "I think the police and Madame Grey must still be questioning Vaughn, but they'll call you soon."

With his rich mother, he'd probably be out of jail in a flash even if they arrested him. He had nothing to worry about.

But why did I have a feeling I'd overlooked something obvious?

I hung up, then called Madame Grey's number.

"Ah, Blair," she said. "I don't suppose you plan on coming to assist me with apprehending this werewolf in person? It seems you were right—he did indeed enlist the help of Mr Wilfred Bloom, in order to cheat his way through his interview with Mr Bayer. He also procured a fake wand from a crafter outside town."

"So that's how he did it," I said. "Uh, I was just on the phone to Wilfred and he said his mother will probably get him out of trouble if it comes down to it."

"I expected nothing less when we bring him in," she said. "Did the wizard admit to anything else?"

"Nope." I shook my head, picturing his puzzled expression as I'd seen through my paranormal-sensing power. "Something didn't quite add up with his account of what he did after the interview, though. I was trying to work out if he went back and killed Mr Bayer after he got caught. I really don't think he has the temperament."

Neither did Vaughn. He'd asked someone to cheat for him, but out of desperation to hide his werewolf nature, not maliciousness.

"Got caught?" she echoed. "The werewolf didn't mention anything about being caught."

"Wait, Mr Bayer didn't catch him in the act?"

Then he *didn't* have a motive. Unless he'd lied, of course.

"There's no way of knowing exactly what transpired in the time between the interviews and Mr Bayer's death, short of questioning all the suspects again. Perhaps Mr Clarke has something to add."

Simeon Clarke. The one candidate I hadn't called since our first disastrous meeting. He'd been interviewed after Wilfred had left, so Wilfred hadn't helped *him* cheat... at least, I thought not. Maybe I should have asked.

I didn't see him. He was gonna interview the last candidate, Simeon whatsit, so I left.

My lie-sensing power had pinned part of his words as the truth and another part as a lie. I didn't know nearly enough about my abilities to know how to fine-tune them, but the part about him interviewing Simeon last was easily provable given the order of the interview results. Which left... the rest of it.

How could Wilfred be so sure he hadn't seen Mr Bayer, yet my lie-sensing power said otherwise? His words had practically oozed sincerity, and yet unless my ability was faulty...

Are you sure? Yes.

What if there was a disconnect between what he believed to be the truth and, well, reality? If my ability could pick up on that subtle difference, then that explained the weird result. What it didn't explain was the truth about what Wilfred had really done after the interview.

And why he believed otherwise.

"Madame Grey," I said. "Can magic make someone forget something?"

"Of course it can," she said. "There are a dozen types of

memory-altering potion alone. Not that it's an easy type of magic to master by any means."

"Unless you have mind powers." Blythe's face came into sharp focus. "Mind reading, mind... control?"

A chill raced down my arms. Mind control... what effect would *that* have on my lie-sensing powers?

"In theory? Yes. As a latent talent, it's a very rare ability."

I bet it is.

"I think you have the wrong guy," I said quietly. "Wait for me—I'll be there as quickly as I can."

I activated my own boots as I left the office, unable to keep myself from feeling like it'd be the last time. I'd left utter chaos behind me, and yet—I'd never forgive myself if I got innocent people locked up.

Before I could second-guess myself, I broke into a run, or hover. The other shops would still be open. It was broad daylight, though the police were otherwise occupied. As I reached Mr Bayer's shop, I slowed down.

Did you kill him? I'd asked Simeon. Without missing a beat, he'd said, *No.*

I ran down the alley, and levitated—higher and higher, until I could see clearly over the fence. The nearest killer plant snapped at me, but I was far out of reach.

In the middle of the garden, sure enough, were the plants with pink-veined leaves, and a large amount of overturned earth.

I descended, knowing what I'd find before I reached it. The buried remains of a spell, hidden in the earth. The spell that blocked mind powers and who knew what else.

And beside them, a person stood beside a suddenly docile-looking killer plant. "You again?"

16

Simeon faced me, his expression calm. Remorseless.

"So it was you," I said. "Only guilty people return to the scene of the crime. That was a stupid idea."

He kicked the ruined spell. "I've been trying to dismantle this blasted thing for a week. He did a thorough job."

"Shame." He wasn't a mind-reader—not that Blythe would have warned me if he was. "Wouldn't want someone to switch off your mind-control ability, huh."

"How did you work it out?"

"I saw you do it to Blythe. It's the only time she's ever submitted to someone." Not strictly the truth, but true enough in hindsight. "Did you wipe her memory or did she just not notice you mind-zapped her?"

"Most people don't. I'm accomplished at using my powers. I didn't even need to use them on you, though. You're nothing."

"I'm honoured." He hadn't needed to mind-wipe me, because it'd taken me far too long to make the connection. After all, the others had looked far guiltier. "Why kill Mr Bayer? Why not join him instead?"

"Because I can't permanently keep someone under my control," he said. "It'd have been a pain to keep him under watch while I stole all his spells, and the other candidates were cheating right in front of his eyes. So I swiped the spell and had Bloom take him out of the picture. He could levitate over the fence in those ridiculous boots of his—which also helped me to dispose of the evidence."

"And then you what, wiped his memories?" Poor Wilfred. Someone would have to break the news to him, but maybe it was kinder to keep him in the dark. Assuming I lived to tell the tale.

"It's better that way," said Simeon. "Like Bayer, he completely squandered his talents. But I stole enough of his props to make up for all the magical skills I'm supposedly lacking."

"And then you came back to finish me off." He was controlling the plants, too. How had I ever thought the other two might be more threatening? He'd nearly killed me once already.

"Sorry about this, Blair. Nobody will find you here." He stepped closer. While we'd been talking, the plants had begun to inch closer to me. "Are you scared?"

"No." My voice didn't tremble—and I didn't fall.

I'd lied.

I *could* lie.

I hit the heel of the boot, levitating out of reach of the snapping plants. *Nice try.* He didn't wear boots of his own, because he thought he didn't need them.

"You can't run from me, Blair."

He raised a hand, doubtless to cast a mind-control spell, and I flew upwards out of the way. The plants moved where he directed, and I moved faster. Flying. I was *flying.* Not levitating, or walking on the air. My body rose higher as though of its own accord.

177

"Get down," he snapped. The plants swayed after him, snapping at my heels. I flew on—right towards a group of stone-like figures rapidly approaching from the air. Three gargoyles, huge and menacing.

"Get him!" I shouted at them, pointing at a now panicked-looking Simeon.

The gargoyles drew closer. Simeon had nowhere to run.

"Should have brought those boots," I told him as the three gargoyles flew in.

Steve the police chief followed close behind, facing me in mid-air. "You're flying."

"Yes, I am. Get this guy behind bars before he uses his mind control ability. The counter-spell is buried in the garden, and I don't think you want to gamble on whether or not it works."

Everyone moved very quickly then. While the gargoyles flew down to surround Simeon, one of them took my advice and dug up the anti-mind spell device. There were doubtless other curiosities buried in the same place, or stolen by Simeon.

"I suppose I should thank you," said Steve the Gargoyle in a gravelly voice, once we'd landed outside the shop.

"Yes, you should," I said. "Considering you can fly. He disposed of the evidence in the garden and put a spell on it preventing anyone else from getting in, which is illegal even when you ignore the fact that he had an innocent man murder someone."

"I searched the garden," he said through gritted teeth. "Of course I knew there were poisonous leaves there."

"And the ingredients for the prototype spell Mr Bayer was working on?"

"There were the ingredients for a million spells, you idiotic girl."

"Don't speak to my employee that way," said Veronica,

walking over to us. "It looks like she did a better job than you did."

Maybe I wouldn't get fired today after all.

"You know your absurd little company has found more criminals than employees," snarled the gargoyle.

"We attract an interesting clientele. Besides, the paranormal world is small." Veronica gave him a smile I couldn't quite read.

"I don't want to point fingers," I said. "But—Blythe's magic is similar to Simeon's. Are they related? Might she have known?"

"I spoke to her already," said Veronica. "She's not an accomplice, but she'd certainly have recognised someone with similar magic to hers. I can only assume she didn't know what he was capable of."

"She didn't," I said. "I mean, she said she didn't know who the killer was, and I'd know if she was lying. He must have hidden his thoughts from her, but he probably recognised her as a mind-reader anyway."

She'd better hope that was true, otherwise the two of them would be seeing each other in the paranormal jail shortly. The gargoyles might have overlooked the obvious, but they were scarily efficient. Simeon Clarke was thoroughly handcuffed, and several witches accompanied the gargoyles when they finally left, with Simeon in tow.

Veronica turned to me. "You were lucky."

I nodded. "I'm sorry for going behind your back and butting into the investigation. I know it has nothing to do with me—"

"It does now. What affects one person in Fairy Falls affects all of us. Including you."

She couldn't have given me a better endorsement if she'd tried.

I smiled. "Thank you."

———

Veronica gave me the rest of the week off to recover from my ordeal. Not that I spent it recovering. My new cat was very demanding, for a start, and there were things to buy and a new home to make mine. I got through to a removal company on the phone and arranged to have the rest of my belongings dropped off outside the town. They were confused when I said to leave the boxes in the middle of nowhere, but I said I'd handle it.

"I'll wear the boots," I said to Alissa. "I can almost fly now."

"You *did* fly when you caught the criminal."

I'd yet to repeat the performance. "Maybe it only works when I'm under stress, or my life is in danger."

Blythe had left the office with her wand permanently bound from casting hexes for the foreseeable future, and there were rumours that Veronica had sent out word for a replacement. Okay, those 'rumours' came from Bethan and Lizzie, who were calling up potential candidates. I was happy to leave them to it, as long as the new witch wasn't a mind-reader.

"Maybe it does," Alissa said, a touch of hesitancy in her voice. "I hope you don't mind, but I asked my grandmother to reach out to her contacts about your abilities."

I blinked. "You mean, fairies?"

"No, the other witches."

"I'm not a witch. The spell was wrong."

"No—it was right. She had to put out feelers amongst the covens… some of them weren't keen to hand over the information, but when pieced together with what I know, it's the only likely explanation."

"Explanation for what?"

"You're one of us." She beamed. "I knew it when I saw you."

I shook my head, frowning. "I'm not a witch."

"Your mother was. Tanith Wildflower was."

My mouth fell open. "I—what?"

"Tanith used to live here as a child," Alissa said. "Before I was born, so I didn't know her. But one day, she disappeared. Rumour had it she fell in love with a stranger and left. That's one rumour. The other is that the man she fell in love with wasn't a wizard or even a man at all. Nobody knows for certain, and no one has seen either of them since then. But only a fairy could have put that glamour on you."

"So you're saying—" I needed to lie down. "My mother was a witch. And my father wasn't human?"

The doorbell rang loudly.

"Essentially." She glanced at the door. "Are you expecting someone?"

"No, I'm not. Unless the boss wants me to come back to work." I got to my feet and walked to the door.

The last person I expected to see on my doorstep was Nathan. "Ah. Hi. How'd you know where I lived?"

"Madame Grey," he said, which was enough of an explanation in itself. "I wanted to apologise in person for how I spoke to you the other day. I know you've had a lot to adjust to—"

"I have." My heart lifted, and I might well have levitated without the boots. "It's all sorted now, anyway. I'm a witch." I wanted to hug him, but he looked nonplussed at my jubilation.

"Is that news?" he asked.

"You heard what Blythe said, right? She was wrong. She was the one who hit me with a spell in that bookshop."

He blinked, then frowned. "She was? As well as hexing Callie?"

181

"Yes. She was probably following me around all week, since she apparently had nothing better to do with her time. Is she in jail, anyway?" If my mind hadn't been spinning with information, I might have conjured up a more interesting conversation topic than my former co-worker, but I was genuinely curious as to whether she'd been locked up or not.

"No," he said, still frowning. "But I didn't know she hexed you. The pack wanted her locked away, but her witch relatives managed to convince Madame Grey to lower her sentence to community service in addition to having her wand bound. I can have a word with her if you like."

I shook my head. "No need. I was just curious, and I thought you'd want to know she lied..." Stop talking, Blair.

"Why would that affect whether you're a witch or not?"

"Never mind. It was a misunderstanding." I smiled cheerily. When he smiled back, a shiver ran down my back, and maybe I couldn't entirely blame the weakness in my knees on anything magic-related. I wasn't even wearing the boots.

"Anyway, I'll speak to you soon," he added.

Alissa grinned at me when I walked back into the living room. "An in-person visit. Let me know when your first date is so I can surreptitiously stalk you."

"I think I might need moral support to keep Blythe out of my hair, since she's not in jail and is probably plotting horrible revenge on me," I admitted. "Anyway, we're *not* dating. I think he thinks I'm slightly unhinged, but oh well." I planted myself on the sofa again. "So where did my powers come from? The witch side?"

"Yes. Tanith came from a powerful line of mind witches. In time, you might even be able to learn to *read* minds."

"Like... oh no."

"Oh no what?"

"We're *related*, aren't we?" I said. "Blythe and me."

"No. Maybe second cousins?"

I winced. "Great. First actual family I've met and they're in disgrace and possibly evil."

"They're not your coven. That's up to you."

"This is… a lot to take in." It was, and now my jubilation had died down a little, I couldn't help but wonder what my mother's life had been like. And where she'd gone. "Why do you think they left me amongst humans and not here?"

She stroked Roald. "I don't know, but the other witches know little about why she left, and where she ended up."

"Yeah…" I trailed off. "Rita must have been right when she said I was wearing glamour. What do I actually look like underneath it? I mean, half a fairy… does that mean I have half a wing? Or one wing?"

"There's a place where you can take the glamour off," she said. "I wasn't going to tell you until we knew for sure… you know, I suspected you weren't a full fairy from the start. You'd have had more reaction to touching metals. There'd have been a lot of differences. Plus, I've never heard of a fairy with your ability to sense what type of paranormal someone is. It sounded more like a witch ability, even if nobody else here can do the same."

"Nobody," I repeated. "My mother was special, wasn't she?"

She hesitated, then nodded. "Yes. But I'm sure you'll be a powerful witch in your own right."

———

With Alissa behind me, I climbed up to the waterfall. Glitter danced off the water, and I ran my hand underneath the spray. A pleasant tingling sensation calmed my nerves.

Then I ducked my head, and, with the boots switched on, I leaned right underneath the waterfall.

"You okay?" asked Alissa.

"I think so." My whole body tingled. I withdrew from the water, clothes dripping wet, and…

She gasped. "Your shoulders."

My hand jumped to where she pointed. Wings unfurled behind my shoulder blades, and I *felt* them, odd extra appendages that seemed alien and familiar at the same time.

I fluttered my wings. My body left the ground for a second, and then pitched forwards into the falls. Spitting out a mouthful of water, I began to laugh.

Okay. I needed to work on the flying part. But I could live with this. I really could.

"How do I turn the glamour back on?" I asked.

"It'll turn back on now you're out of the waterfall."

I ran my fingertips across the wing's edge. After a few seconds, they blinked out of existence. I twitched one shoulder blade, which felt weirdly empty. "Maybe I'll try again later."

"Take your time."

I shrugged one non-winged shoulder. "I don't know how I should feel. I'm not sure I want to walk around with the wings out."

"People won't judge you here."

"I think I need a little longer to get used to being para-normal at all."

But I was adjusting. I had a new home, a place where I mattered, and now I had someone to live up to—even if I didn't yet know what had happened to my family. But I'd find them. Someday.

I stepped away from the waterfall. "Let's go back."

ABOUT THE AUTHOR

Elle Adams lives in the middle of England, where she spends most of her time reading an ever-growing mountain of books, planning her next adventure, or writing. Elle's books are humorous mysteries with a paranormal twist, packed with magical mayhem.

She also writes urban and contemporary fantasy novels as Emma L. Adams.

Find Elle on Facebook at https://www.facebook.com/pg/ElleAdamsAuthor/